"You just never knew the real me, Mr. Seymour."

Helen forced a tight, angry smile. Matt's expression darkened ominously.

"And my brother did, I suppose."

"I don't know what you're talking about."

He laughed harshly. "Oh, come on, Helen. I've got eyes. Tim is the spitting image of Steven at that age. You'd been going around with my brother for months before you left Ellermere. Everyone knew you adored him. We wondered why you and your aunt left in such a tearing hurry, and now we know, don't we?"

Helen stared at him. Perhaps she ought to have expected him to come to that conclusion, but foolishly it had never entered her head. He was still watching her furiously and she caught her breath.

"Tim is not Steven's son!"

English author **Kathryn Cranmer** was born in Yorkshire, in close proximity to the moors made famous by the Brontë Sisters, though she did not dream of writing in her early days. On her first job on the staff of a public library she met her husband-to-be. She and her husband have two young sons, and her writing at present is confined to the hours the boys are in school. She loves to travel and she and her husband enjoy swimming, walking and other active pursuits, as well as art, the theater and ballet.

Books by Kathryn Cranmer

HARLEQUIN ROMANCE

2517—PASSIONATE ENEMIES
2620—PAS DE DEUX
2719—WRECKER'S BRIDE

These books may be available at your local bookseller.

Don't miss any of our special offers. Write to us at the following address for information on our newest releases.

Harlequin Reader Service
901 Fuhrmann Blvd., P.O. Box 1325, Buffalo, NY 14269
Canadian address: P.O. Box 2800, Postal Station A,
5170 Yonge St., Willowdale, Ont. M2N 6J3

Secret Lover

Kathryn Cranmer

Harlequin Books

TORONTO • NEW YORK • LONDON
AMSTERDAM • PARIS • SYDNEY • HAMBURG
STOCKHOLM • ATHENS • TOKYO • MILAN

Original hardcover edition published in 1985
by Mills & Boon Limited

ISBN 0-373-02767-2

Harlequin Romance first edition June 1986

CHAPTER ONE

HELEN knew she ought to have been in bed an hour ago but there was something infinitely reassuring about sitting in front of a blazing fire, the gas lights bubbling gently in the background, hearing the snow storm whistling furiously outside the tiny cottage. The small room was very cosy with its colourful rugs and bright cushions, Helen's favourite books lining the shelves, the uneven, white-painted walls hung with pictures and vivid tapestries. She yawned, stretching, the graceful, sleepy movement of a particularly contented cat. Her slim body arched, her outline in tight jeans and a blue sweater undeniably feminine, the warm, rounded curves belying the delicate bones, the frail, almost boyish shape of her pale cheeks and short, blonde curls.

She pushed herself to her feet now, walking over to the window and pulling back the curtains. It had stopped snowing, she realised, the sky was a clear, cold blue, moonlight making the distant line of hills as bright as day. But the wind was still as strong, blowing the feathery snow into huge, white drifts against the garden walls. She and Tim had only cleared the paths at tea time but the work they had done had already been completely obliterated.

She dropped the scarlet curtain back into place with a small sigh. It was fun being snowed in for a day or two but she hoped it wouldn't last too long. Tim had missed school again today and they were rapidly running out of fresh food, but thank goodness there was still plenty of bottled gas left in the cylinder, she thought as she walked into the kitchen to fill the old whistling kettle and put it on the stove to boil, and wood was no problem. The ancient oak which had blown down and blocked the road in the autumn had been a godsend. It had supplied both her and her neighbours with sufficient fuel to last the entire winter. Mr Williams and his son had borrowed a tractor and hauled the dead tree up to the cottages and they had all taken turns at chopping it into logs.

Helen smiled to herself as she remembered Tim's excitement when Mr Williams had allowed him to wield the axe for a short time. Fell Cottage was heaven to him at any time but he had particularly enjoyed the week the tree blew down. In fact, he loved everything about the Lake District. He was obviously a country child at heart and the open fires and gas lights simply added to the charm of their little home. Helen had thought long and hard before moving from Manchester but now she was glad she had taken the plunge. Tim had hated living in the big city. He had hated the crowded, noisy school he was forced to attend. Hawksmoor Primary suited him much better. There were only twelve other pupils in his class and his work had improved tremendously in the last two years.

The kettle boiled and she made a mug of tea and carried it into the living room to drink, standing in front of the dying fire. Then she checked that the door was securely locked and put the spark guard around the fire and she was just walking towards the stairs when she heard the front gate creak as though someone had pushed it open.

She paused instantly, one foot on the bottom step, her body tensed, her ears straining to pick up any further noise. She knew it was probably only the wind that had loosened the catch but stupidly she was nervous. She had always realised that she and Tim could be vulnerable, living alone, so far out of the village but normally it didn't worry her too much. Mr and Mrs Williams were marvellous neighbours. She knew she could call on them for help at any time but unfortunately they were away in Barrow at the moment visiting their daughter.

She waited, listening, her brows an anxious line over her blue eyes. There it was again! Helen was sure now that someone or something was moving about outside the cottage. She crept towards the door on silent feet, trying to ignore the fact that her legs were trembling, shaking uncontrollably, trying to ignore the violent hammering of her heart against her breastbone.

She froze, her ear to the wooden panels, scarcely breathing, so that when the knocking started she recoiled violently away from the door. There was something totally horrifying about standing there, listening to that disembodied noise from the direction of the porch. She ought to have spoken of course. Asked who was there. But her throat had closed up with fright. She doubted whether she would be able to get the words out.

The insistent knocking was still going on, a violent tattoo of sound, as though whoever was on the other side of the door was becoming increasingly angry and impatient. Helen stood in the same spot, turning her head in jerky, panic-stricken movements, searching for something, anything that might conceivably help her to defend herself. It could be anyone outside that door, she realised, a murderer or a rapist. The thought terrified her. But even so when her eyes lighted on the poker she moved towards it slowly, almost reluctantly, picking it up in one sweating palm and hefting its weight against the other.

She had no idea whether she would be able to use it, but if someone tried to break into the cottage she knew she would have to try. There was no way she would allow anyone to hurt Tim, not without a fight. The thought of her nine-year-old son, asleep in bed, stiffened her resolve. She moved back towards the door clutching the poker tightly in one hand.

'Who's there?' she cried. At least she tried to, but her voice came out in a harsh wavering croak and the hammering continued so she said it again, louder this time: 'Who's there? I've no intention of opening this door unless you have a very good explanation to offer. I should warn you that I have a gun and if you attempt to break in I shall use it. I'm a very good shot.' The wobble in Helen's voice rather spoiled the effect of her brave words. They sounded weak and blustering to her own ears instead of aggressive, besides being totally untrue, but at least they provoked some reaction from outside.

The knocking stopped and for a brief moment there was silence so complete that Helen felt sure she could hear the intruder breathing. Harsh, gasping intakes of air which scared her almost as much as an overt threat of violence would have done.

'For Christ's sake!' The exclamation came suddenly, harshly, muffled by the heavy door between them. 'I'm not a burglar! I didn't come up here to attack you! I was looking for the Williams' cottage . . .'

'They live next door,' Helen stammered. She felt ridiculous shouting through the closed door like this but there was no way she was going to open it. There was something about the man's voice, muffled though it was . . . something that she recognised, something that set the alarm bells ringing wildly in her head. 'I expect they're in bed,' she added now, crossing her fingers behind her back, excusing herself for the deliberate lie. Let him go and hammer on the Williams' door until he was blue in the face, she didn't care. She just wanted him to go away as quickly as possible. She heard his sigh through the heavy panels.

'Look, I'll go and waken them up, but I've got my daughter here with me. She's ill. I was taking her into Lyndale hospital but the Range Rover skidded on the way down Cop Hill.' He was talking rapidly, an edge of desperation to his tones. 'Let me leave Katy with you,' he begged. 'I promise I won't trouble you for long. It's freezing out here and she's had a raging temperature.'

Helen didn't reply. In fact she was incapable of speech, struck dumb with shock as she collapsed weakly back against the wall, the poker sliding from her suddenly nerveless fingers. This couldn't be happening to her, it just couldn't! But it was, and the urgent voice on the other side of the door was reminding her of that fact in no uncertain terms.

'For God's sake, woman!' he groaned. 'I've got a child here who might be dying! Doesn't that mean anything to you? If you still think I'm crazy enough to have walked all the way up here in the teeth of a snowstorm to rape you, look out of the window. I'll bring Katy round so that you can see I'm telling the truth.'

Helen moved her head slowly backwards and forwards against the wall, gasping for air, trying to dispel the weakness, the horrible sick feeling in the pit of her stomach. She had no need to go to the window. She had recognised the owner of the voice and she knew he was telling the truth. Although she had never seen Katy Elisabeth Seymour in her life before she seemed to know almost as much about her as she did about her own son. How could this have happened? The one man in the world she had hoped never to meet again and he was standing on the other side of the door from her. Why had he come? Why had fate played such a filthy trick on her? Her world had been safe and contented, but suddenly, in the space of a few seconds it had crashed in ruins around her feet.

'For Christ's sake!' Matt Seymour was thumping on the door again and Helen pulled herself together with an effort, her fingers trembling as she struggled to turn the heavy key in the lock. It had a habit of sticking and it did that now so that she had to press her weight against the door before the lock would turn.

Katy's father was pushing past her before she had properly widened the gap. A tall, indistinct figure muffled up in an old sheepskin, a blanket-wrapped bundle clutched in his arms. He carried his burden over to the small sofa, setting it down gently, and as Helen walked across the room behind him still in a state of shock, he was removing the cream blanket, pulling the wet cap off the child's head, dark curls tumbling over the arm of the sofa.

'I'll go straight round and try to rouse Mrs Williams if you'll watch Katy until I get back.' He was speaking quickly, over his shoulder without looking at Helen, his gentle hand smoothing the dark hair from his daughter's forehead. 'If she can't breathe, if she has another attack when I'm out, lift her up a little, it seems to help.' He watched Katy for another moment, his brown eyes anxious and then he sighed. 'I'd better go . . .'

Helen had been standing to one side, her pale face in shadow, watching his lean capable hands as they dealt so gently with his small daughter. He had been far too busy to pay any attention to her and she was grateful. It had given her chance to collect her thoughts, chance to fight off the ridiculous urge to run and hide before he could take a proper look at her. And a moment's rational thought had told her that she couldn't allow him to go next door. Mrs Williams was away. If he knocked all night he wouldn't get any answer, and he would think she was crazy when he discovered the truth.

'There's no point in going out again,' she said quietly. 'Mr and Mrs Williams went into Barrow yesterday and they're not due back until the day after tomorrow.'

'Oh God!' he sighed. He still hadn't looked at Helen. His dark eyes were fixed on his daughter's flushed face as he sank back on to his knees at her side, despair in every weary line of his body. 'I knew Mrs Williams had brought up a large family of her own. I was hoping she would have some idea what was wrong with Katy.'

Instinctively Helen moved closer, bending so that she could see the child's face without having to touch the man at her side. Katy was asleep, eyes closed, face flushed, her breathing still sounding uncomfortably loud and harsh in the small room. But after looking intently at her for a moment Helen didn't think she was seriously ill. It was difficult to tell with children of course and after a momentary hesitation she placed her hand on Katy's forehead. It was hot and slightly damp and as though the touch of Helen's fingers had disturbed her, Katy moaned softly, her small body twisting restlessly in sleep. Helen's face softened and suddenly it no longer mattered that this was the daughter of Matt Seymour and his wife. Katy hadn't even been born the last time Helen had seen Matt. She oughtn't to be made the scapegoat for her father's past misdeeds. She was just a small, sick child who needed help and Helen knew that was how she had to try and think of her.

Helen straightened abruptly on the thought. Maybe she didn't have Mrs Williams' experience with children but she could see that for Katy the first priority was warmth and dry clothing. She began to move towards the stairs, her tones brisk as she spoke to Matt over her shoulder.

'I suggest that you take off your own wet coat and start to undress Katy. I'm going to fetch some dry blankets and a pillow from the linen cupboard, we'll make Katy more comfortable before we decide what else can be done.'

Matt seemed relieved to be able to do as Helen suggested. It was clear that although he loved his daughter the present crisis was beyond his experience. 'I'll do my best,' he said, turning a faint, grateful smile in her direction and Helen forced a quick, bright answering smile and hurried on her way upstairs, relieved to be out of Matt Seymour's disruptive presence if only for a few minutes.

But even though he was no longer standing so solidly in front of her she couldn't keep him out of her thoughts and bitter-sweet memories jostled alongside equally unwelcome questions as she searched rapidly through the linen cupboard. Just what were Matt and his daughter doing here? It was the middle of the night; why had he felt the need to travel all the way to Lyndale hospital? Surely with all the resources the Seymour family had at their disposal he could have found help nearer at hand? And just where was Katy's mother? Surely Natalie would want to be with her daughter when she was ill? Any mother would.

Helen's thoughts were still fully occupied when she hurried back downstairs, her arms piled high with blankets and pillows, a pair of Tim's clean pyjamas clutched in one hand.

Matt was still crouching at his daughter's side. He had taken off Katy's coat and shoes as well as his own sheepskin, but his hair was still slightly damp, Helen noticed, and inches longer than he used to wear it, dark strands brushing his collar at the back. She walked towards him slowly, reluctantly across the threadbare carpet and he must have heard her coming down the stairs because some of the treads were loose and they creaked abominably, but only now did he turn towards her.

'She's still asleep,' he murmured, his tones low and husky. He was looking at Helen but she sensed that in his head there was room for no one but Katy and that suited her. She only hoped the situation stayed like that. She didn't want him to see her clearly. Ten years was a long time. She had changed. But had she changed enough? Would he recognise her? That was the question, and at this moment she didn't want to speculate on the answer. She moved forward, trying to force her tense muscles to relax, trying to behave as though he was a stranger whom she had just met for the first time this evening.

'I've brought a pile of blankets and a sheet, and there are a couple of pillows if you want to make up a bed for your daugher on the sofa whilst I put her into a pair of my son's pyjamas.'

She didn't wait for his reply. She scooped Katy up into her arms and carried her over to the chair at one side of the fire. Compared to Tim the girl's slender body was as light as a feather. She was still asleep, her head resting against Helen's shoulder, dark strands of hair clinging to her damp forehead. There was something incredibly intimate about holding Matt Seymour's daughter in her arms like this and Helen had to force herself to concentrate on the purely physical task of slipping the cosy top and trousers over the child's slender figure.

When she had finished Matt was still struggling to make up a bed on the sofa and she couldn't resist watching him covertly over the top of Katy's head. Tall, dark and handsome was a hackneyed phrase but it still applied to Matt. He was all she remembered him to be and more. He and his brother had always possessed the kind of smooth good looks which were faintly unbelievable and if anything maturity had added to Matt's dark attraction, the slightly haggard look he was wearing at the moment adding an extra dimension to his lean, tanned features. The love and concern he felt for his small daughter mirrored in the depths of his warm, brown eyes.

She had to remember exactly what he had done to her, Helen told herself sternly, turning her eyes away. Maybe he hadn't changed in the last ten years but surely she had! She was no longer the naïve, unsophisticated sixteen year old who had walked away from Ellermere House. Surely she had learned her lesson by now? Matt was dangerous. She mustn't allow the strange circumstances of their meeting to affect her judgement. Above all she must keep cool, maintain her composure. She lowered her head, her cheek against Katy's fragrant hair and when she raised it again Matt was beside her, leaning down to take his daughter from her arms. He placed Katy on the makeshift bed, tucking the covers gently under her chin, and very much against her will the tenderness in his expression touched Helen deeply.

'I don't think you need to worry,' she murmured, feeling a ridiculous urge to reach out and comfort him. 'I'm fairly certain that she's not seriously ill. My son had croup a couple of years ago and the symptoms were very similar to Katy's. Whatever it is, the crisis seems to have passed. I think she needs rest and sleep more than anything.'

Matt sighed, pushing himself to his feet, one hand raking through his thick, dark hair, his eyes still lingering on his daughter's restless form as though he couldn't bear to turn them away. 'I'm sure you're right. She is looking better and her breathing is definitely easier now. I ought never to have brought her out this evening but I'm afraid we all panicked. It was almost impossible for her to breathe. She sounded as though she was dying,' he murmured, his brown eyes clouding as he remembered his earlier fears.

'Sylvie, the girl who normally looks after Katy, has gone home to Switzerland on holiday, the telephone wires from the main road to the house were down and road conditions were worsening by the minute, we decided that the hospital at Lyndale was the only place for her. The Range Rover is usually very good on icy surfaces but I'm afraid I was too concerned about Katy, my mind wasn't on the road ahead. I was careless coming down Cop Hill and we went into a skid at the bottom.'

Matt's quiet words had answered some of Helen's unspoken questions, but she still wondered why Natalie's name had never been mentioned. Surely they weren't divorced. But no, that was a ridiculous idea, she realised instantly. Matt and Natalie had been ideally suited—a handsome, charming, intelligent couple. There must be some other explanation, but Helen had no intention of asking. She couldn't do so without betraying herself. Besides, every minute they sat and talked like this increased the risk of recognition. She had to get away from Matt as quickly as possible.

'You've had a worrying evening,' she said with a

sympathetic smile. 'Katy will still need attention tomorrow so I suggest that you use my bed for tonight and I'll stay downstairs and keep an eye on her.'

Matt was far from happy with her suggestion. He shook his head. 'I wouldn't hear of it. We've already imposed on you far too much.'

'I was pleased to be able to help,' Helen insisted, not altogether truthfully.

He was still smiling, his dark eyes faintly teasing. 'I was glad you didn't decide to shoot me anyway.'

Helen could feel herself flushing, her delicate features burning with vivid colour. 'You could have been anyone,' she protested, half angrily and he nodded.

'I know it and I'm sorry, but believe me at that moment in time I was far too worried to concern myself with anyone but Katy. I must have given you a terrible shock, I do realise that. I can only apologise again and hope that you'll be willing to forgive me.'

'It's okay, I understand,' Helen murmured, half reluctantly. She tried to keep her voice cool but it was difficult when he was looking at her with such a warm expression. Why did he still have to be so damned attractive? Why couldn't he have put on weight during the last ten years, lost his hair and his strong white teeth? Surely at the age of thirty-five there ought to be some discernible difference? Helen reflected ruefully.

He was still smiling. 'It's kind of you to say so. My name is Matt Seymour by the way ...' He raised his dark brows, holding out his hand as he spoke and without thinking Helen put hers into it.

'My name's Delaney, Helen Delaney,' she murmured, not quite meeting his eyes and he shook his head watching her with a puzzled expression.

'I was sure we'd met before, but the name doesn't ring any bells I'm afraid.'

A log fell into the hearth behind them, angry red sparks flying in all directions but Helen barely noticed, she was too busy wondering whether she ought to tell him the truth or not. Her head was bent, soft curls clustering in her nape, but she could sense that his eyes were still on her. His curiosity was aroused. She ought to have known that it would be impossible to keep her identity a secret. Even if he didn't remember her now, he would do so later and then what would his reaction be if she hadn't told him the truth?

She raised her eyes. 'We have met,' she conceded reluctantly. 'I used to be Helen Morley. I lived at Ellermere House for a time when my aunt worked for your mother.'

The words sounded so calm and ordinary somehow and yet they hid so much pain and heartache it seemed impossible to Helen that she could say them so unemotionally. But fortunately Matt couldn't read her thoughts. He was staring at her in total silence, an expression of almost comical amazement on his handsome features. But Helen had never felt less like breaking into laughter. He was too close. His eyes were too intent and before she could guess what he intended and take avoiding action he had reached out and taken her hands, pulling her closer to the light.

'My God, I simply don't believe it,' he muttered, moving his head from side to side in a slow gesture of incredulity. 'Helen, little Helen Morley, after all these years.'

He was standing clutching her fingers and Helen tugged feebly, attempting to pull them away without it being too obvious, but he was holding them far too tightly for that so she stood there, trying to ignore the touch of his cool flesh against her own, knowing it was impossible.

'I'm sorry, Helen,' he was saying now. 'You must be furious with me. I ought to have recognised you immediately, but this is the last place I expected to see you.' He paused, his smiling gaze sliding appreciatively over her. 'On second thoughts perhaps my lack of recognition isn't so surprising. You've changed! My God, how you've changed!'

There was no doubting the meaning of Matt Seymour's words and Helen had to force herself to stand and endure that smiling glance when all she longed to do was walk away, turn her back on his tall, self-confident figure. I'm immune! she told herself fiercely, keeping her own smile pinned to her lips with a supreme effort of will. Matt's charm was as natural to him as breathing and it meant nothing. Surely she ought to know that by now?

Matt was still holding her hands and Helen was so busy fighting her own silent battle that he had pulled her half way across the room towards one of the shabby armchairs almost before she realised it and when he gestured for her to sit and took the chair opposite her, she obeyed him automatically, too disturbed to even utter a token protest.

He was leaning forward now, his hands hanging loosely between his knees. 'Tell me all your news,' he begged and Helen's self-confidence took another nose-dive. He looked like a man with a thousand questions—all awkward ones that she wouldn't be able to answer without telling deliberate lies. His sudden appearance at her door tonight had been bad enough, but this was worse. She had too many secrets and she was terrified that Matt would uncover them. She hated not being able to tell the truth but what alternative had she? And Matt's first words simply confirmed her worst fears.

'How long have you been married, Helen? Is your

husband here with you?' Matt's questions came thick and fast and not for the first time Helen blessed Philip's insistence that she invent a mythical husband, weave a believable story of unhappy marriage and divorce, for Tim's sake if not for her own. Matt believed everything she told him without question and the fact that he believed her lies gave her added confidence. She began to relax, her taut body uncoiling in the seat, her slender hands which she had been clenching and unclenching in her lap, halting their unconscious movement.

She discovered that it was easy to talk to him about her life in Manchester. She didn't have to tell him any lies about that. Certain omissions were necessary of course. She made no mention of the first painful months after she and Aunt Lily had left Ellermere. It wasn't something she would have been willing to discuss with anyone, least of all Matt Seymour. She had been distraught, living in a world of grey shadows. It was fortunate indeed that her aunt had obtained a position as housekeeper to Philip Ackroyd. She saw now that it had been his undemanding kindness, both before and after Tim's birth which had helped her through those unbearable months.

An elderly vicar, widowed himself for many years, he could have been shocked by Helen's predicament. But no, there had never been any hint of criticism in his manner towards her, and yet he had seen, as Helen had not, the problems that she and Tim would encounter when they eventually left the vicarage and tried to make their own way in the world.

Helen kept on talking, telling Matt what he wanted to hear, all the time busy with her own disturbing thoughts. It was only when he began to talk himself that she felt compelled, almost against her will, to listen. She had been telling him about Tim and he was smiling at her, his dark eyes holding a mixture of amusement and incredulity in their depths.

'Amazing! Little Helen Morley, a mother! I still can't believe it. It doesn't seem two minutes since you were a child yourself, following Steve and me around in the holidays, all gawky legs and plaits, determined not to be left behind. Do you remember?'

Helen nodded, not trusting herself to speak. She remembered all too clearly. She was afraid she would never forget. Memories were insidious things. You thought you had them firmly under control but then something unexpected happened and there they were, rushing back at top speed to haunt you all over again.

Matt was still talking, painting a vivid picture of those halcyon days when she had been young, before her hopes and dreams had been shattered. It was ironic really, Helen reflected, watching Matt with shadowed eyes. He appeared to have an almost photographic memory when it came to the most trivial incidents from the past, but her own most painful and lingering memory from that time he had completely forgotten.

'Steve's in New York now, did you know?' he asked and Helen shook her head mutely, watching those beautifully shaped lips framing words to which she didn't want to listen. The past was dead. Her memories of it were painful enough, she didn't want to talk about it as well. But clearly Matt had no such inhibitions.

'We expanded into the States about five years ago and he went out to handle that side of the business. You wouldn't recognise him now,' Matt said with a grin. 'He married an American girl a couple of years ago and he's totally domesticated. He was upset when you left Ellermere so suddenly, Helen. You had made quite a hit with my little brother. In fact it was a shock to us all,' he added now, his dark brows raised in silent question. 'One day you were with us and the next you'd disappeared. I don't think my mother ever did discover exactly where you'd gone.'

Helen's shrug was a careless as she could make it. 'Aunt Lily was offered a job in Manchester. She was born there. Her friends and family were there so it was natural that she should want to accept it. I don't believe we left in that much of a hurry. I'm sure Aunt Lily gave the necessary number of weeks notice.'

'I'm sure she did, too, but it was a shock all the same.' His next words were softened by the faintly teasing smile he gave her. 'We'd grown used to having you around the place. We'd begun to think of you and Aunt Lily as permanent fixtures.'

His words were said jokingly but that was exactly what she and her aunt had been, Helen reflected bitterly—part of the furniture as far as the Seymours were concerned. They had left a gap when they fled, but it had soon been filled. Matt had not even recognised her this evening, Helen thought, forgetting for a moment that a few minutes ago she had considered that an advantage.

'How is your Aunt Lily, by the way?' Matt asked her now. 'Is she still living in Manchester? I know my mother would welcome news of her.'

'She's dead,' Helen responded flatly. She leaned back in her chair, slender legs stretched out in front of her, thinking of her aunt. Lily Morley's heart had given out almost three years ago, hard work and worry having taken their toll. It still hurt Helen to talk about her death but today the words had come out almost without a pang. Her brain had sustained so many shocks during the last two hours that it felt numbed, as though it was stuffed with cotton wool, her nerves and emotions completely blunted.

'I'm sorry,' Matt said gently, watching her face. 'I know how close you were.'

'She was all I had. I owed her everything.' Helen's voice was husky with emotion as she said the words. Her debt to Aunt Lily had been immense. She could never have repaid it if her aunt had lived to be a hundred. For a brief moment the small Lakeland cottage and the silent, masculine figure sitting opposite her might never have existed. Helen was completely absorbed in her own thoughts and strangely it was her mother's face, rather than Aunt Lily's, that intruded now, a sudden vivid image of Emma Morley's beautiful face raised in quiet laughter to the man at her side. That had changed of course, both the beauty and the laughter, after Helen's father had left. Charming, handsome and feckless, he just hadn't been able to take the prolonged demands of domesticity. Helen had never heard her mother utter a word of blame but year by year she had seemed to fade away a little more, until in the winter of Helen's eighth birthday – she had contracted pneumonia and died.

That was the first time Helen had ever met her mother's sister and she remembered the moment of Aunt Lily's arrival in her life very clearly. She had been alone in the living room of the small, shabby home she and her mother had shared. She could even recall the clothes she had been wearing at the time: they were black, because that was the day of the funeral; an appalling black skirt and jumper which didn't fit, both borrowed from well-meaning neighbours. She had stared at Aunt Lily, frozen faced and dry-eyed, as she walked through the door. She had been in the same state ever since her mother's death. The neighbours had been shocked by her lack of emotion but fortunately Aunt Lily hadn't shared their feelings, seeming to

realise without being told that Helen's grief was too
deep for tears; grief and fear as she wondered what
would happen to her now that her mother was no
longer alive to care for her.

'I'm Lily Temple, your mother's older sister,' she told
Helen gruffly. 'Refused to see her after she married that
fool of a husband . . . made a mistake. I didn't realise
what a bad time she was having.'

Helen had realised later that her aunt often spoke like
that, particularly in moments of emotional stress. Short,
sharp bursts of sound. Almost as though the words
were an embarrassment that she wanted to get rid of as
quickly as possible. But embarrassment or not she had
taken Helen back with her to the Seymours' house and
Ellermere had been her home for the next eight years.

Helen stirred, sighing faintly, wondering just how
long she had been sitting there lost in thought. Matt
was leaning back in the armchair, his face half in
shadow and he was silent too, but he looked across at
her now as though the small movement had disturbed
him and she flinched from the sympathy she saw in his
eyes. He knew the story of her childhood, he no doubt
realised she had been locked in painful memories but
compassion from him was hard to take. She didn't want
him to be kind to her. It would have suited her far
better if he had been harsh and unsympathetic, because
that was how she wanted to see him.

'Okay, Helen?' he asked quietly and she nodded
wearily, wishing she had the courage to tell him to go to
hell, mind his own business. It was his probing
questions which had reawakened her unhappy memories
but he didn't seem to realise that. 'So you live here
alone with your son?' he asked now and Helen nodded,
her voice as calm and cool as she could possibly make it
as she replied.

'Tim was unhappy in Manchester. I saw the cottage advertised a couple of years ago and we've rented it ever since.'

Matt was still watching her closely. 'Aren't you lonely? It's a long way out of the village, no electricity or mains gas . . .'

'No, we couldn't be lonely,' Helen denied quickly. 'Not with Mr and Mrs Williams as neighbours, and I soon got used to the minor inconveniences. Anyway, Fell Cottage is all I can afford. We were lucky to find it. Most cottage property in this area is snapped up as a holiday home the moment it comes vacant.'

'And a damned nuisance that is,' Matt agreed, his mouth taking on a sudden downward curve as he answered her. 'It makes things very difficult for the young people who were born in the area. I don't own much property myself, but when anything does become vacant I make sure it goes to local people.' He paused now, as though weighing his next words, watching Helen from beneath thick, dark lashes.

'In fact I do have a couple of cottages vacant at the moment,' he said at last. 'Just outside Whingate. I have a prospective tenant for one but the other is still free. The rent is far from exorbitant. It has electricity, there is no gas but there are open fires in both downstairs rooms. Why don't you and your son take it? It's only two miles from Ellermere.'

Perhaps Helen ought to have seen where Matt's words were leading but in fact his suggestion had taken her completely by surprise and she stared at him for a moment in complete silence. He was smiling, looking well pleased with himself whilst her own reaction was one of growing horror. Living two miles from Ellermere in one of Matt Seymour's cottages! The thought made her shudder.

'It's very kind of you . . .' she stammered at last.

'It's not kind at all, Helen. It would give me great pleasure to be able to help you.'

Helen bent her head, soft curls framing her cheeks and forehead in a delicate halo of gold. 'It is kind of you,' she insisted quietly, shock still making her voice tremble a little. 'I don't want you to think that I'm ungrateful, but I can't accept. Tim's settled here—we both are. It would mean a new school for him, new friends, new neighbours and he's at an age where he needs security and a settled existence. Besides which the cottage is ideally placed as far as my work is concerned.'

'I was going to ask about that. Surely opportunities for employment in the village are limited?'

He raised his dark brows and Helen relaxed, leaning back, her head turned towards him, pleased to have changed the subject with so little difficulty. A neutral topic of conversation at last. One of the few subjects she could discuss with Matt Seymour and not have to invent lies or give evasive answers.

'I'm an artist,' she explained and his brows rose even higher.

'Really, I had no idea.'

Matt was hiding his incredulity well but Helen's lips twisted into a faint, wry grimace of amusement. 'Incredible, isn't it? Particularly when you remember the pathetic results I achieved as a teenager.'

Matt shook his head. 'Some of your pictures were good. My mother still has the water-colour you painted of Coniston Water hanging in her sitting room.'

'Your mother was always very kind, but there's no need to pretend, Matt. I know that most of the work I did in those days was pretty awful. I'm no genius now,' she added with a deprecating shrug, 'but I've been very fortunate. The vicar who employed my aunt after we left Ellermere was a keen artist. He saw some of my amateur efforts and encouraged me to do more. He said I had an undeveloped talent, which quite frankly I didn't believe. But he managed to bully me into attending the local art college. I eventually graduated. He then helped me to find an agent and slowly commissions for artwork began to materialise.'

'As the man said, you must have had the talent to begin with.'

Helen pulled a small face. 'Maybe, but I would never have used it without his encouragement. I'm grateful now, of course, but at the time I was as obstructive as I could possibly be. He never let up. He really hounded me until I did as he wanted.'

And she had given in at last, Helen remembered, her eyes gentle beneath their thick fringe of lashes, but it had been with an ill grace. All she had wanted to do then was bury her head in the sand like an ostrich and hide herself away from a world which she knew had treated her badly. Philip had realised exactly how she was feeling, of course and he had been determined to make her start living again. He couldn't make her forget the past but he had done the next best thing. He had shown her that she could cope in the present. She had health and strength and he expected her to use the small talent she had been born with, to carve out a new life for herself and Tim. And amazingly she had succeeded. She lifted her head and looked across at Matt Seymour.

'That's all there is to tell,' she murmured and Matt lounged back in his seat, watching her.

'The last ten years in a nutshell?'

Helen nodded, a faint smile curving her lips. 'I'm afraid so.'

'And your ex-husband, is he an artist too?' Matt asked.

Helen's lips kept on smiling but inwardly she sighed. Here we go again! More of Matt Seymour's awkward questions. He seemed adept at choosing them. Almost as though he knew the truth and was deliberately baiting her.

'He isn't an artist,' she replied quietly. 'He's an engineer. He completed his training at Manchester University and we met when he was there. But he's in Saudi Arabia now, working on an oilfield.'

Matt leaned forward as though he was going to question her again but Helen had had enough. She shook her head, lifting one slender hand to brush back the soft tendrils of hair falling over her forehead. 'No,' she protested trying to shape her lips into a teasing smile. 'We've talked quite enough about me. Surely it's your turn now.'

He raised his hands. 'I'll do my best. What do you want to know?'

'How about everything,' Helen replied and he laughed.

'As simple as that.' But Helen sensed a reluctance to speak almost as great as her own and then told herself that she was being oversensitive, Matt Seymour had nothing to hide. Why would he be reluctant to talk about the past?

'Where do I start?' he asked. 'What would you like to hear first?'

'Well, we heard that you'd married Natalie and we saw the notice of Katy's birth in *The Times* but I'm afraid we lost touch after that,' Helen responded brightly. They had lost touch deliberately but she didn't intend saying that to Matt. Reading the news of Katy's birth had torn her apart, reopened wounds which she had thought were healed. That had been the moment when she had decided to bury the past, forget the Seymours completely. Until now!

She looked across at Matt and wished that she could

turn back the clock a few hours. Had she known what was going to happen she would have turned out the lights and gone to bed at nine o'clock this evening. Completely ignoring him when he hammered on the door. But it was too late for such wishful thinking. He was here and she would just have to make the best of it. He was speaking quietly, a husky, pleasant murmur. Helen hadn't been listening, but his next words pierced even her self-absorption.

'I presume you don't know that Natalie's dead?' And as Helen paled visibly, shaking her head in shocked surprise Matt added, 'She died in the States two years ago.' His tone was low, betraying none of his feelings and Helen stared at him in silence, too horrified to say anything for a moment.

'Matt, I'm so sorry,' she whispered at last. 'I didn't know.' Beautiful, sparkling Natalie, dead. It was unbelievable. She'd been about the most alive person Helen had ever known. Silky, dark hair swinging around the perfect oval of her features, she had seemed to dance light-heartedly from one exciting day to the next. How had it happened? Helen wondered. Had she been ill or in an accident? Looking across at Matt's shuttered features Helen knew she couldn't ask. Obviously the subject was still too painful for him to discuss. It didn't surprise her. Natalie was not easy to forget. She bit her lip, wondering what to say to break the small, uncomfortable silence. But she need not have worried, Matt broke it himself, his tones quietly pensive as he stared into the dying flames.

'We moved back to Ellermere after my wife died, Katy and I. It seemed to be the sensible thing to do. My father had suffered a fatal heart attack a few months before Natalie's death. Mother was lonely. Her health has never been her strong point and she depended on my father a great deal.'

'I'm sorry, Matt,' Helen murmured, wishing she could stop feeling so concerned for him. It was unsettling and not the way she wanted to think of him at all. 'I was very fond of your father. He was very kind to me,' she added quietly.

'He was a good man,' Matt agreed, the hard planes of his face softening as he remembered. 'And I know he loved you dearly, Helen. We all did.' He leaned forward, his hand closing over her fingers with warm, compelling strength. 'It must have been fate that brought me to your cottage tonight. We were meant to meet,' he told her huskily. 'And now that I've found you we must never lose touch with each other again.'

CHAPTER TWO

HELEN went to bed soon after that, climbing the stairs and sliding under the covers to lie shivering, her teeth chattering, for what seemed like hours, listening to the wind whistling round the cottage, hearing the tiny creaks, the rustlings, the familiar but unidentifiable noises as the old house settled down for the night. She only wished that she could settle down as easily. But no matter how desperately she burrowed beneath the duvet it was impossible to still the hyperactive turmoil in her brain. Matt's parting words were still ringing in her ears, and she knew he had meant every one of them. He was determined that they should see each other again and at this moment Helen couldn't think of any way to stop him.

Ironically the niggling worry that she might bump into one of the Seymours again had been her one reservation about moving back to the Lake District. But it hadn't happened. She had thought she was safe. She had thought that at last she had escaped from the past. How wrong could she have been! Escape was impossible! The memories had been there all the time, waiting to be resurrected. Just the sound of Matt's voice outside her door had been enough to bring them flooding back and unfortunately it was never the things you wanted to remember that came into your mind at times like this.

When Matt had walked into her tiny cottage this evening she had tried to concentrate on all the reasons she had for hating him, making herself remember how

30

ten years ago he had hurt and humiliated her, almost destroyed her life without even realising it. But instead her thoughts had slipped irrevocably back to the time when she had first arrived at Ellermere. She knew she had been an odd, withdrawn child, but all the Seymours had been kind to her and from the very first meeting she had adored Matt and his brother Steven.

They were like beings from another planet to Helen. Handsome, intelligent, sure of their own world and their rightful place in it. She had tagged along behind them whenever they arrived home for the holidays and amazingly they had never seemed to resent her. She must have been an appalling nuisance and yet they had shown remarkable tolerance. And lacking a family herself she had basked in the warm, friendly atmosphere at Ellermere.

'That's child's just like a puppy,' Helen remembered Mr Seymour saying on one occasion. 'Every time I turn around, there she is, watching me with those big, blue, hopeful eyes.' His voice had been half impatient, half amused and Helen had been hurt at the time but looking back she realised the truth of George Seymour's words. She had been the family pet, following the Seymour boys around with her big, adoring eyes. Waiting for them to show their approval. Grateful for any scrap of attention they were prepared to give her.

And slowly that unthinking adoration had grown into love, bringing its own problems, problems which Helen realised she simply couldn't bear to think about, not tonight, not with Matt Seymour drowsing downstairs in the fireside chair. It made her memories too immediate, too painful. Instead she closed her eyes, willing her tense body to relax. And although she didn't expect to sleep, as she grew warmer her eyelids began to droop and when she opened them next it was to the cold, grey light of a new morning.

She saw from her bedside clock that it was still early but she stumbled out of bed anyway, shivering as the icy chill of her bedroom struck through her ribbed pyjamas. She washed quickly, trying to make as little noise as possible so as not to disturb Tim. She had already decided that he would have to stay in bed until Matt and Katy had left. She couldn't risk them meeting, either today or in the future. And whatever Matt said to the contrary she had no intention of allowing him to visit Fell Cottage again. It would create an impossible situation.

Hurriedly she dressed in the same jeans and blue polo necked sweater she had worn the day before, sitting in front of the dressing table mirror and brushing her short, blonde hair with brisk, vigorous strokes, the silky curls emphasising the fragility of her heart-shaped face, deepening the vivid blue of eyes which seemed to dominate the rest of her features. Ten years ago when she had left Ellermere Matt had not recognised that she was already a woman but from the way he had stared at her yesterday evening, all that had changed. Whether he was still grieving for Natalie, or not, she had still seen the gleam of purely masculine interest in his eyes when he had looked at her. She would have to get rid of him as quickly as possible this morning and make very sure that he never felt the faintest desire to return. But how was she going to do it? And she was still musing over the problem when she eventually crept out on to the landing and quietly pushed Tim's bedroom door open.

He was still asleep and she stood for a moment, feeling a sudden, inexplicable lump in her throat as she stared down at him. He was lying on his back, his cheeks lightly flushed in sleep, his dark hair standing out in tufts around his face as though his sleep had been a restless one, and as she watched, his eyelids lifted, revealing eyes as large and vividly blue as her own.

'Morning, Mum, it it time to get up?' he muttered drowsily and he started to push himself up on his pillow with one elbow until Helen thrust him firmly down again.

'No,' she whispered, bending over so that her mouth was close to her ear. 'Stay where you are. The weather hasn't improved during the night. It will mean a walk into school again today so I think you had better have another unscheduled holiday.' He had suffered a number of feverish infections recently which had left him feeling under the weather and Helen told herself that she was quite justified in keeping him away from school for another day.

'Great!' He was smiling, still sleepy. 'I'll get up anyway and help you with the breakfast.'

'Stay in bed for now, love,' Helen insisted quietly. 'I'll bring some breakfast upstairs a little later.' He was looking puzzled and she explained rapidly. 'Someone had an accident on Cop Hill last night. A man and his daughter. They're downstairs at the moment and you know how it is in the living room. We'll all be falling over each other's feet if you come down as well.'

He accepted her explanation without surprise. With just one tiny room the cottage sometimes seemed crowded with only the two of them in it. 'Who is it? Do we know them?' he asked now, bright-eyed with interest.

'You don't but I have met the man before. Don't worry, I'll tell you all about them later,' Helen promised with a smile, bending to tuck him under the duvet again. 'And I'll bring your breakfast up as soon as I can, okay?'

He nodded quite happily and Helen left the room and hurried quickly down stairs, her footsteps barely muffled by the threadbare carpet covering the treads. The cottage had been let fully furnished and that had suited Helen. She couldn't have afforded to furnish even this small house from her own resources and even the shabby carpets and lumpy furniture were better than nothing.

She reached the bottom of the stairs and stepped into the room, noticing that already the curtains had been pulled back from the windows letting in the pale, morning light, the fire was crackling cheerfully and there was a faint, aromatic smell of coffee drifting towards her from the open kitchen door. As she hesitated, Matt Seymour himself walked out of the kitchen, a blue mug, presumably containing coffee, clutched in one hand. He looked wide awake this morning, very tall, very broad, his white shirt opened at the collar beneath his dark sweater. He hadn't been able to shave of course and the dark stubble on his chin gave him a faintly rakish air as he smiled across the room at Helen.

'I hope you don't mind,' he murmured, his voice low so as not to disturb his daughter, still asleep on the sofa. 'I took the liberty of using your kitchen. Katy's still asleep, but I thought I'd have a coffee now and then go straight down to the car, see if I can manage to dig it out.'

'Don't you want any breakfast?' Helen asked, schooling herself to speak naturally as she crossed the room towards him. She wanted to go into the kitchen but he was still lounging in the doorway and she had to squeeze past him, holding herself stiffly to avoid making contact with his indolent figure.

'I wouldn't mind some toast when I get back, if that's okay?'

Helen was in the kitchen now, she glanced around and he was smiling at her, his dark eyes shadowed by those ridiculously thick lashes. He took a sip of coffee, still watching her over the rim and she looked away immediately.

'Of course,' she agreed a little too quickly. She was feeling far too aware of him suddenly, knowing that her foolish reaction was in itself a warning. The bread bin was nearly empty but that was a minor consideration at the moment. Helen knew that she had to get rid of him, and fast. She began to move around briskly, picking things up and putting them down again, not really knowing what she was doing.

'You're running out of milk I'm afraid.' His voice came from close behind her and she had to steel herself not to flinch away. 'If I can get the Rover on the road, I'll take Katy home and come back here afterwards, ferry you into the village to do your shopping.'

'It's very kind of you, but I have plenty of tins in store. We shan't starve, don't worry, thanks anyway.' Helen opened a cupboard door, took out a packet of tea and closed it again with controlled violence.

'It wouldn't be any trouble. I noticed there was no car outside. It's one hell of a walk up that hill from the bus stop, carrying parcels.'

'We manage. Tim helps me,' Helen replied. They did have a car at one time but it seemed to be continually breaking down. In the end she had to let it go. She simply hadn't been able to afford the money for repairs. But that didn't mean she wanted any help from Matt Seymour.

'Ah yes, where is that young man this morning? Oughtn't he be to getting ready for school?'

The kettle whistled and Helen poured boiling water into the teapot, taking a mug down from the cupboard above her head. 'He's not going to school today. He's had 'flu recently and the buses won't be running. I don't want him to walk into the village.'

Matt was silent for a moment but she could feel his eyes on her as she poured milk from the bottle into her scarlet mug. She was so tense she wanted to scream aloud. Go away and leave me alone! Stop talking! Go and dig out your blasted car and take Katy back to Ellermere. But Matt seemed completely unaware of her mood.

'I was going to ask you to have lunch with me later,' he murmured reflectively and Helen took a trembling breath.

'I'm sorry, I can't leave Tim.'

'I do realise that. But perhaps we could make it dinner later in the week. If you can't get anyone to look after your son I feel sure my mother would be pleased to do it.'

Helen took a sip of scalding coffee, her back still towards Matt Seymour, knowing that the hand holding the cup was trembling and hoping desperately that he hadn't noticed the fact. The dreadful thing was that if his name hadn't been Matt Seymour, if the past hadn't been looming between them, she would have been strongly tempted to accept his invitation. He was an attractive man, and this morning, as yesterday, he was choosing to exert all his considerable charm. But it wouldn't do, of course. It didn't bear thinking about and Helen was secretly horrified at her own weakness. There was no way she could brush the past aside and she was a fool even to think such a thing. Matt was still waiting for her answer and she shook her head, her soft curls gleaming gold in the pale sunlight flickering through the kitchen window.

'Tim hates staying with strangers, I'm afraid.'

'Then bring him over for tea as soon as the weather improves. I know my mother would like to see you again and it would give Tim an ideal opportunity to get to know her.'

Helen put down her mug carefully on the wooden drainer. 'That's very kind of you Matt, but I'm afraid it simply won't be possible.'

He gave a short, half impatient laugh. 'Oh come on, Helen, I'm sure the boy would enjoy himself and so would you,' he added huskily, a cajoling note deepening his tones. 'It would be just like old times. Don't turn me down.'

Helen had begun to realise that whatever she said Matt simply wasn't going to take no for an answer. And yet she had to make him accept her refusal. She didn't want to see him again, she told herself firmly and she certainly couldn't allow him to meet Tim. Why then was she being so polite to him? Why didn't she just tell him frankly and brutally how she felt? She was sure that receiving a brush-off would be a new experience for him. It would be a blow to his ego. One that she doubted he would ever forgive and surely she would never be troubled by him again!

She turned slowly to face him, knowing just what she had to do but finding it amazingly difficult to put her silent resolution into practice. She raised her eyes, deliberately meeting his warm, brown gaze, forcing a cool, confidence she was far from feeling into her tones as she said: 'I'm afraid the answer must still be no. It was kind of you to invite me but I can't accept, not today, or next week. I'm sorry to be so blunt but the truth is I don't want to come out to dinner with you.'

Matt had just raised his arm to take another sip of coffee but now he lowered his cup, placing it with studied care on the work surface at his side, his firm lips partly open as he stared at Helen, all the warmth and charm fading slowly from his face.

'I don't want to be rude,' Helen continued, well launched on her cruel theme, forcing herself to ignore the stunned expression on his face. 'But I'm afraid that my situation here and the fact that we had a slight acquaintance in the past may have given you the wrong impression. I was happy to be able to help you and Katy last night. Who wouldn't have been? And it was pleasant to renew our acquaintance and reminisce briefly about the past, but that's as far as it goes I'm afraid. I'm not particularly sentimental, nor do I feel nostalgic for events which took place more than a decade ago . . .'

As Helen uttered her stilted little speech she realised that practically every word was a lie. But she had to carry on, she had no choice and it certainly seemed to have the desired effect. Matt's jaw had tightened ominously and his eyes were dark, icy pools, filled with cold contempt.

'I see,' he stated curtly and the brief words made Helen wish that the floorboards would open and swallow her up.

'I'm sorry,' she whispered, unable to continue her cool charade a moment longer.

'Not at all,' he responded in glacially polite tones which were far more daunting than a spurt of righteous anger would have been. 'You did try to be tactful. The fault was entirely mine. You must forgive me, I'm not usually so insensitive to atmosphere. Put it down to worry over Katy combined with lack of sleep. If you would excuse me now I had better see to the car.'

Without another word he turned his back and strode across the room, picking up his coat on the way. Helen was in no doubt as to his feelings. His lean body seemed to throb with suppressed violence and the quiet click as he closed the outer door was almost as betraying as a violent slam would have been.

After he had gone Helen felt sick. She leaned against the draining board, her eyes closed, her legs shaking, wondering how she'd had the courage to look him in the face so brazenly and say the things she had. One thing was certain, if his parting expression was a true indication he wouldn't be paying a return visit. He would take Katy home as soon as he could and that would be the last she would see of him. Helen began to move around the kitchen slowly, preparing Tim's breakfast with only half her attention. She had done what she set out to achieve, she told herself bracingly. She had taken the only course possible. Why then didn't she feel happier about it?

It was some time later that she became aware of the quiet sounds from the direction of the living room. Matt's hasty departure must have woken Katy she realised. She knew the child would be frightened and bewildered, finding herself in a strange house and she also knew that she ought to go in to her but it was a few more minutes before she felt she had mastered her emotions sufficiently to walk into the room.

As Helen had expected, Katy was sitting up staring around, her brown eyes bewildered, her lower lip trembling just a little as she realised that her father was nowhere in sight. Helen felt ashamed of herself now for hiding in the kitchen. The child had been ill. She was frightened. It wasn't her fault that her father and Helen had quarrelled. Helen walked across to the sofa smiling warmly, her own worries pushed to the back of her mind as she sought to soothe the small girl's fears.

'Good morning, Katy. Your father's just gone out to see if he can get the Range Rover into commission again. You skidded into a ditch yesterday evening, do you remember? Your father carried you here wrapped in a blanket.'

Helen fell silent. Katy was watching her with huge, anxious eyes and Helen would have liked to take the child in her arms and cuddle her but there was something about the stiff little figure that told her Katy would resent this. She was near to tears but clearly determined not to show it. She wouldn't thank Helen for her sympathy right now.

'I don't know you.' Katy's figure was still tense but Helen thought her explanation had helped a little.

'No you don't' she quickly agreed. 'My name's Helen Delaney. I have a son two years older than you, but he's in bed at the moment recovering from an infection.'

'Oh.' Katy absorbed that, relaxing visibly, staring about her now, her bright eyes very curious. 'Do you live here all the time?'

Helen nodded.

'The lights are funny.'

Helen laughed. Katy was interested now and had clearly forgotten to be frightened. 'They're gas lamps. We live too far out of the village for electricity to be installed so instead we have gas delivered a few times a year in containers. We have gas lighting, a gas fridge, even my iron is fuelled by gas.'

'Can you get gas television, too?' Katy asked, her small, oval face wearing a serious expression.

Helen laughed again and shook her head. 'I'm afraid not, but we do have a portable set that runs on batteries.' Helen's words seemed to reassure the child. She smiled, two dimples appearing in her pale cheeks.

'I like it here.' She pushed her feet from under the blankets, Tim's pyjamas hanging over the end of her toes so that she waved them in the air, giggling.

'Those belong to my son,' Helen told her.

'Will he mind me wearing them?'

Helen shook her head.

'Can I see him?'

'I don't think that's a very good idea,' Helen replied gravely. 'Tim's had flu and still isn't completely recovered. You've been ill yourself and although I can see that you're feeling better this morning, I wouldn't like you to catch any more germs. Your father wouldn't be very pleased with me, would he?'

Katy thought for a moment and then nodded, obviously seeing the point of Helen's words. 'Will my daddy be long?' she asked, hopping off the sofa.

'I don't think so. It hasn't snowed again in the night. Unless your car has been damaged he ought to be able to dig it out without too much difficulty,' Helen said, mentally crossing her fingers. 'Would you like to get dressed and have breakfast while you're waiting for him?'

Katy agreed cheerfully, her earlier fears completely forgotten and when Matt finally slammed back into the house thirty minutes later, Katy was washed and dressed again in the blue sweater and corded trousers she'd been wearing when she arrived, sitting at the small dining table just polishing of the last of the boiled egg and toast that Helen had prepared for her. She turned her head the moment the outer door slammed, smiling, dark curls bobbing as she scrambled off her seat throwing herself straight into her father's arms.

'Daddy, Daddy,' she squealed. 'Tim has two pet rabbits and a hamster and he keeps them in the outhouse. I've had a look at them and they're lovely. Can I have some rabbits to keep if I promise to look after them myself? Can I, Daddy? Can I?'

This was all said in an excited, breathless rush, but

Matt stopped her before she'd finished, his curt voice cutting off her excited words.

'If you've finished your breakfast, thank Mrs Delaney for looking after you so well and put on your coat and shoes. We shall have to be going.'

'But Daddy, what about the rabbits? I want you to see them,' Katy wailed.

Matt's mouth was tight. 'Later, Katy.'

'Now, Daddy, now!' Katy was tugging at his sheepskin coat, clearly not accustomed to her father denying her anything she wanted.

'Later, Katy,' he reiterated sternly, disengaging her clinging hands and moving her gently to one side. 'Now, where are your coat and shoes? Your grandmother will be waiting.'

Helen was already on her feet. She'd draped Katy's duffle coat over the back of a chair beside the fire. It was warm when she picked it up, which was more than could be said for Matt's eyes when at last he had looked at her. It had only been a brief glance but it had made her shiver and her fingers were shaking as she helped Katy into her outdoor clothes, wrapping her in the grey duffle coat and crouching in front of her to lace the small brown shoes as quickly as she could.

'The snow's too deep for these. You'll get your feet wet.' It was a relief to look up into Katy's bright little face. She had quickly swallowed her disappointment about the rabbits and was smiling cheerfully again now.

'Daddy can give me a piggy-back,' she grinned, clearly relishing the prospect.

'That will be nice.' Helen stood up slowly, reaching for the cream blanket that Katy had arrived in. 'Are you going to carry this, Katy?'

'I'll take that.' Matt moved suddenly past his daughter, firmly removing the blanket from Helen's

limp fingers. He was very close and instinctively she
looked up at him, drawn by his momentary stillness,
wincing as she encountered the expression in his dark
brown eyes. 'I'm sorry we troubled you, Mrs Delaney,'
he muttered tightly. He would clearly have liked to say
much more but Katy was a very interested spectator,
her wide eyes watching them both curiously. 'I'll see
that you are compensated . . .'

Helen flushed deeply. 'That won't be necessary,' she
retorted sharply. 'I was pleased to be able to help.' He
was deliberately trying to humiliate her, she realised.
She had wounded his self-esteem and he was
determined to pay her back in her own coin.

Matt placed his hand on his daughter's shoulder. 'Say
goodbye to Mrs Delaney, Katy.'

Helen looked down at the little girl, trying to smile,
afraid to raise her eyes in case she encountered Matt's
icy gaze again. Katy's arms reached up towards her and
instinctively Helen dropped to her knees, hugging the
small, childish body, her face buried for a moment in
Katy's sweet-smelling curls. Ridiculously she felt very
near to tears. 'It's been lovely to meet you, Katy,' she
whispered huskily, very conscious of Matt's tall, sternly
brooding figure at her side.

'Thank you for the boiled egg and for showing me
Tim's rabbits. Will you tell him that I've been?'

'Yes, of course I will, love.'

'Do you think he'll let me come and look at them
again? I could bring some lettuce leaves and things from
the kitchen. Mrs Ellis will give me them if I ask.'

'That will depend on your daddy, Katy.' Helen
pushed herself slowly to her feet. She hated to see
Katy's face change, the smile fading slowly as she
sensed the reserve in Helen's answer. But much as
Helen liked the little girl she didn't want a repeat visit.

'We'll leave you then.' Matt's voice was brusque and he turned abruptly, walking towards the door, the blanket under one arm, pulling Katy along with the other.

Katy hung back, her eyes on Helen. 'I'll see you soon, Mrs Delaney.' But she no longer seemed quite so certain.

'Goodbye Katy,' Helen murmured gently.

Matt's dark head half turned, nodding briefly, not really looking at Helen as he reached the door. 'Goodbye, Mrs Delaney.'

The coldly formal words had an air of finality which Helen told herself was exactly what she had wanted to achieve. Matt picked Katy up in his arms and began to stride through the crisp snow and Helen stood at the door watching until they were out of sight. Katy's little face turned back towards her, her gloved hand waving, was the last glimpse she had of them before they plunged into the narrow belt of trees bordering the road.

CHAPTER THREE

HELEN allowed Tim to get up as soon as Matt and his daughter had gone. She sat at the small dining table and ate her breakfast—or tried to eat it. Her appetite seemed to have deserted her. Reaction had set in. Her stomach was churning and one look in the bathroom mirror had told her that she was deathly pale, her blue eyes feverish in their brilliance. She took occasional bites of her toast, listening with half an ear to Tim's chatter, her thoughts still with her departed visitors.

Katy was a delightful child. Like Tim she was very mature for her years, brought up in that vast house with her grandmother and the housekeeper as her main companions it was hardly to be wondered at. Helen would have liked to see her again but knew it was impossible.

'Mum, hey . . . come back to earth.' Tim's cheerful voice penetrated Helen's thoughts at last. She turned to him, smiling.

'Sorry love, I was miles away. What were you saying?'

'I was asking if you were going to do some work today?'

Helen sighed, propping her chin on one hand. 'I ought to go into the village and do some shopping.'

'The bus won't be running, not yet.'

Helen sighed again. 'I know it.' The hill out of the village was precipitous and although the bus drivers did their best, it was just too dangerous for them to negotiate in heavy snow and ice.

'Did Mr Seymour get his car out okay?'

Tim's words echoed Helen's thoughts so exactly that she jumped, recovering herself quickly. It was stupid to allow herself to dwell on Matt Seymour and his daughter like this. They had made a brief, unwelcome incursion into her life and now they had gone and she had to banish from her mind just as completely.

She shrugged faintly. 'I think so, I know Mrs Denton never has problems with her Range Rover. She seems to battle through whatever the conditions.'

'I think he might have offered to give you a lift into the village. He must have realised we were running short of food.' Tim had eaten the slice of toast Helen had left and was carrying the dishes into the kitchen. Helen watched him, her head still propped on one hand.

'I don't suppose he gave it a thought, Tim. He was very grateful and he did offer to leave some money.' Helen felt a pang of guilt as she was saying this but brushed it aside again quickly. Matt had offered to take her shopping but that had been before she had told him a few home truths. He hadn't volunteered again after that she'd noticed and besides she had carefully avoided telling Tim too much about last night's visitors. She didn't want questions. She didn't want to talk about them. She just wanted to forget they had ever existed.

But she could see Tim was still anxious to discuss the same topic and she pushed herself to her feet now, smiling with bright determination. 'I don't feel much like working today, at least, not inside. It's a beautiful morning. Would you like me to pack some sandwiches and a flask? We could take a walk up to the ridge. It's ideal weather for photography and I might even manage some sketching.'

Tim was enthusastic, his pale face lighting up. 'That would be great, Mum. I could try out that new film I bought.'

Tim had recently developed a passion for photography and he had produced some quite interesting pictures. Helen thought he definitely had talent and she was keen to encourage it. Tim washed the dishes and then went to bank up the fire while Helen packed sandwiches and filled a small flask with coffee.

She had always encouraged her son to help with the household chores. She wanted him to learn to be independent. There was no man by her side to lend her support. If anything happened to her he would be alone. It was a frightening thought but it helped a little to know that in practical matters at least, he would be able to cope. Emotionally of course, it was another matter. Everyone needed love and who would give it to Tim if she wasn't there? As always when the question filtered into Helen's brain she pushed it out again very quickly. She was being morbid, she told herself sternly. She couldn't control the future. She could only give Tim as much love and attention as possible now and hope for the best.

She put the cheese sandwiches into the rucksack with the flask and a couple of apples and then began to get ready herself. She dressed quickly in a blue quilted anorak, pulling waterproof trousers over her jeans and a knitted cap over her short curls. She looked far from elegant, but her clothes were warm and practical. The sun might be shining but the cold wind could be a killer to anyone foolish enough to venture on to the hills without adequate protection.

Tim had already disappeared to feed his rabbits and she went outside to join him, the rucksack swinging over one shoulder, her face upturned; enjoying the frail warmth of the winter sun. Tim came running as soon as he saw her, his usually pale cheeks flushed from contact with the crisp, cold air. The sky was a vivid blue over their heads as they climbed the hill behind the house, the snow crisp beneath their feet. Tim forged ahead, laughing as he planted giant footsteps in the smooth, glittering surface.

Helen watched him, smiling to herself as his scarlet-coated figure disappeared into the trees ahead of her. He was a happy boy. Maybe she hadn't been able to give him very much in the way of material possessions but he was secure in her love and that was the important thing. She followed Tim into the forest, her feet crunching through the frozen snow. It was very still and silent under the trees, the branches weighted down by snow. Tim's red-coated figure striding ahead, providing the only bright colour in that enclosed white world.

They climbed for an hour through the stands of sessile oak and the tall fir trees, the snow underfoot making it hard going in places. But at last they came out into the open again and stood, shading their eyes against the glare, looking back the way they had come. The cottages were invisible from here; lost in the trees; protected from their harsh environment by one of the last remants of wild forest which had once clothed the whole of the Lakeland fells.

They climbed higher, struggling now against the icy wind, Helen's cheeks burning pink with cold and they reached the ridge at last, looking down the length of the valley, the lake in the bottom reflecting the blue of the sky, the serrated thrust of the Langdale Pikes forming an impressive backdrop.

Tim took his photographs and they found a sheltered hollow out of the wind, sitting on the waterproof Helen had carried with her to eat their sandwiches. And later she tried to sketch as Tim strode about, looking for new angles and scenes to photograph. Helen's pencil moved over the paper. She even produced a picture of sorts, but her mind was not on her work. She looked again at the uninspiring lines on the white paper and instead saw Ellermere as it had been the summer of her sixteenth birthday. At that moment the picture was so vivid she could have painted it from memory. The old, stone-built house set on a hillside above the lake, surrounded by trees and carefully maintained gardens. She could even remember the smell of the gardens. Mrs Seymour had collected old-fashioned roses and they had been in riotous blossom the June of that year. Branches dripping with pink and purple flowers, their perfume heady, seeming to invade the whole of the house.

She had done a great deal of walking in the Ellermere gardens that summer, she remembered. Usually hand in hand with Steven, the younger of the Seymour boys. They had had fun together, playing tennis, swimming in the lake. Aunt Lily had of course muttered dire warnings which Helen had ignored. Helen's eyes softened as she remembered. Dear Aunt Lily, she knew that life often wasn't kind, particularly not to women on their own. Hard work and poverty had taken their toll of her own strong body, turning her beautiful hair from glossy black to iron grey, etching bitter lines on her once handsome features. Helen realised now, when it was too late, that her aunt had loved her deeply. She had wanted the best for her niece. She had believed that the Seymours, however kind, would not want a permanent relationship to develop between their beloved son and the cook's daughter.

But Helen knew she was in no danger from Steven. It was Matt, the older brother that she loved. The two boys were good friends; they went everywhere together. If she stuck with Steven she got to see Matt. It was as

simple as that. She knew she had no chance with him.
He still saw her as a gawky adolescent. In his eyes she
still hadn't grown up. But just to be with him was
enough. He was kind to her. His glamorous girlfriends
tolerated her and so Helen continued to date Steven
whenever he asked, hiding the way she felt about Matt
so well that even his brother never guessed.

It had been an evening in August when Helen's life
had changed so dramatically. They were invited to a
party just outside Ambleside, herself and Steven, Matt
and his girlfriend, Natalie Demaine. She and Steven
had gone on ahead and the party had been in full swing
when Matt had finally arrived on his own.

Helen had seen him the moment he walked into the
house. He smiled at her but there was something in the
glittering brown eyes which told her he was furiously
angry and when Steven took her hand and pulled her
towards his brother, Matt's words had confirmed
Helen's suspicions.

'Natalie and I are finished,' he grated when Steven
asked where she was. 'That's it! I've had enough! She can
go and whistle somebody else to heel. It won't work
with me again.'

Helen never discovered exactly what he and Natalie
had quarrelled about because he stalked off then,
prowling the crowded rooms like a handsome,
predatory tiger. Helen followed his progress through
the evening with anxious blue eyes. He flirted and
danced his way through the night with a kind of
reckless determination and his mood seemed to unsettle
his brother. Steven drank more than he was accustomed
to and gradually the alcohol began to take effect. Helen
had increasing difficulty holding him off. She had let
him kiss her before but his mood tonight was wild, his
mouth when it claimed hers was hungry, his hands

moving over her body in a way that alarmed her. However much she protested he wouldn't take no for an answer.

She was fighting him off in a corner, her face flushed, her blonde hair dishevelled, when Matt strolled up, seeing what was happening at a glance. 'I'm taking Helen home,' he told his brother abruptly, detaching Helen from Steven's embrace with apparent ease.

Steven squared up to him belligerently. 'Like hell you are!' he flung back angrily. 'I'll take her home myself when I'm good and ready.'

'You're drunk,' Matt stated frankly in an even, unemotional tone which seemed to inflame his brother's temper further. 'You are not fit to drive. You can either come with us now, or I'll drive back later to collect you. Which will it be?'

Helen trembled in the protective circle of Matt's arms. Steven looked angry enough for anything and she could feel the tension in Matt's stiff body as he waited for his brother's reply.

Steven glared furiously at them both for a moment, swaying on his feet. 'Neither, damn you,' he muttered. 'I'll drive myself home. You're welcome to take Helen. She's a frigid little tease. I'm going to find myself someone who is warm and willing ...' He wandered off, his face sulky, totally unlike the man Helen thought she knew.

She had cried a little in the car going home, her head turned, trying to hide her tears from Matt. But he had seen her distress and without saying anything stopped the car in one of the quiet parking spots beside the lake, taking her in his arms, his mouth in her hair.

'Don't let that idiotic brother of mine upset you, sweetheart,' he murmured comfortingly. 'He's drunk. He doesn't mean what he says.'

Helen buried her face in his shirt and clung to him in seventh heaven, Steven's cruel words completely forgotten. Perhaps he sensed her instinctive response because within minutes the comforting arm around her shoulders had tightened and one firm hand turned her face towards him as he began to kiss her. Helen was in a hazy dream which she never wanted to end. Her arms slipped around his neck and she kissed him back as she had wanted to do so many times before.

'Sweet Helen. Sweet little Helen.' He murmured that to her over and over again. Helen sensed something odd about his manner even then, but she was too deliriously happy to change her response. It was only when his kisses became more demanding, his hands roving more boldly over her body that she tried to resist, Aunt Lily's warnings floating to the surface of her dazed brain.

'Don't, Matt, please,' she begged and he raised his dark head, breathing hard, his eyes as dazed as her own as he stared down at her soft mouth trembling so desirably. 'You're so beautiful, Helen,' he groaned thickly. 'Let me make love to you?'

His hand was on her thigh as he spoke, stroking, caressing her soft skin, evoking sensations in the pit of her stomach that she had never felt before, exciting sensations she wanted to go on and on, but which at the same time scared her half to death. He kissed her again, his hard mouth greedy on her own, touching the skin of her neck and shoulders, his hands thrusting down the straps of her simple cotton dress, smoothing her flesh with searching, restless fingers until Helen was on fire, her whole body suffused with damp, feverish heat.

She moaned as his hands touched her bared breasts, ashamed of herself for allowing the small sound to escape but unable to prevent it. She knew she ought to be fighting him but she seemed to have no strength to resist. He was murmuring husky, passionate words of love as his mouth travelled over her heated skin, his voice hoarse, his breathing as wild and ragged as her own as he stared pleadingly into her dazed blue eyes.

'Let me love you, Helen . . . please,' he begged and Helen couldn't resist that look or the deep, husky tone of his voice. She loved him. She had always loved him. Her arms curved around his neck as she kissed him back without restraint, her mouth as urgent as his own, her body arched against his in passionate surrender.

He had taken her then, his hands rough on her slender body as though his self-control had finally snapped completely. Helen didn't enjoy the sensation. He hurt her and it took an immense effort of will for her not to burst into tears. As for Matt, once the rather brutal act of love was finished he seemed almost to forget that Helen was in the car with him. They drove home in silence, Matt peering through the windscreen as though he was having difficulty seeing the road ahead. And when they reached Ellermere he stumbled up to his room still without a word, leaving Helen to cry herself to sleep that night. But still she had loved him—although she almost dreaded meeting him again. What if he despised her for giving in to him so easily? What if he regretted making love to her? She was frightened of seeing Matt and yet waiting desperately for him to come to her. Next morning it was hard hiding from Aunt Lily how she felt. She was in the kitchen helping to make Sunday lunch and every time the door opened her head shot up, her eyes automatically turning in that direction.

When Steven walked in at last she flushed up to the roots of her hair. Because of what had happened afterwards she had almost forgotten how Steven had behaved, the things he had said to her. But she remembered them now. Almost as tall and dark as his brother, he stood in the open doorway, looking faintly uneasy. 'Could I have a word with you, Helen?' he asked. His tone was uncharacteristically tentative and Helen had carried on chopping vegetables with feverish concentration for a moment. She didn't want to speak to him. For the first time in her life she felt embarrassment when he looked at her. But sensing the curious glances Aunt Lily was throwing in their direction she had followed him outside at last.

They stood in the kitchen garden, shielded from the house by the tall rows of beans the gardener had planted. It was a hot, sunny morning and the droning of the bees flying in and out of the orange flowers was almost deafening. They faced each other, Steven still looking uneasy, his face very pale, his eyes bloodshot with dark circles under them.

'I'm sorry about last night,' he said at last, raking one hand through his dark hair in a faintly nervous gesture. 'I'm afraid I don't remember all that much about it. But I do recall that at some point you were having to fight me off.'

Helen blushed and he sighed apologetically. 'What can I say, except that I'm sorry? I hadn't had that much to drink, but apparently Dave Thornton decided to have some fun last night at my expense. He doctored my beer ... Matt's too, I'm afraid. I've got one hell of a head this morning but Matt's in a worse state than I am.' His pale lips twisted into a faint grin as he added, 'He's still in bed and he threw the alarm clock at me when I went into his room to see if he was okay.'

'He could have killed you both! What if you had had an accident going home?' Helen was horrified. How could anyone play such a pathetically childish trick, she wondered and for the moment the other implication of Steven's words escaped her.

Steven nodded, agreeing with her. 'Dave didn't think of that until this morning apparently and then he panicked and confessed everything to Jeff. I've always thought he was a fool but in this instance I guess he had his reasons.' And when Helen looked bewildered he added, 'He was swanning around with Natalie Demaine before Matt came on the scene. According to Jeff he was crazy about her. Matt can't be his favourite person at the moment. Natalie's been trying to get her claws into my brother for months and since she succeeded Thornton hasn't had a look-in.'

'What did he use? What did he put in the drinks?' Helen asked quickly. The thought of Natalie Demaine with her claws in Matt was not one she wanted to encourage, particularly not today.

'God knows! His father is a doctor.' Steven shrugged. 'I wouldn't have thought there would be drugs left lying around but I daresay it wasn't too difficult for Thornton to get hold of what he needed. In fact he refused to tell Jeff what he had used. "It won't have killed them," was his only comment. But by all accounts he was pretty worried. As he had every right to be. Jeff ran me home last night himself or I suspect that I would certainly have ended in a tangled heap at the side of the road.'

Helen accepted Steven's apologies graciously but she knew things would never be the same between them again. Too much had happened. She felt like a different person today. She returned to the kitchen and carried on with her chores, her face averted from Aunt Lily's shrewd gaze. Matt would come to see her as soon as he had recovered, Helen knew that. But the day dragged on and he didn't appear and when Helen met him at last it was quite by accident as she was carrying a dish of salad into the dining room for the Seymours' evening meal.

Helen stood gazing at him, her heart in her eyes, the wooden salad bowl still clutched forgotten against her chest. He was wearing a pale blue shirt, opened to reveal the tanned, muscular column of his neck, but his face was pale above it, deep shadows beneath his dark, expressive eyes.

'Hello, young Helen,' he said. 'Brother Steven tells me I ran you home last night.' He laughed then, shaking his head. 'You had a lucky escape, my love. I don't remember a blessed thing about the journey home. It's fortunate that car of mine knows its way without any assistance.'

He was on his way out to the garage, the car keys dangling from one lean finger and Helen watched his departing figure, the colour draining slowly from her cheeks, leaving her as white as a ghost. Only gradually, over the days that followed, did it dawn on her that he had no recollection of the events of that evening. At first she thought he might be regretting his actions, pretending his mind was a blank. But eventually she accepted that he had been so dazed by the alcohol and drugs he had inadvertently consumed he had genuinely forgotten everything.

She had loved him even then, perhaps secretly hoping that the brief attraction would somehow be rekindled. A week later Matt's engagement to Natalie Demaine had been announced. Helen had crept around the house like a little white mouse after that. She had given herself to a man who clearly didn't care a damn about her. It had been so unimportant to him that he didn't even remember making love to her. She was only sixteen but she was growing up fast. Even so, two months later when she discovered that she was pregnant she doubted if she would have been able to cope without her Aunt Lily's help.

Aunt Lily had been angry and distressed, as much with Matt Seymour as with Helen and she was adamant that the Seymours ought not to discover what had happened. 'We want no charity from them,' she'd snapped at first when Helen had tentatively suggested that course of action. 'And if you're thinking Mr Matt would marry you and give Natalie Demaine the push, think again, love.' And then she'd looked at Helen's stricken face and shaken her head. 'Well ... maybe I'm wrong. Maybe he would do just that. But would you want him on those terms?' She gripped Helen's shoulders, giving them a tiny shake.

'Think a minute, love. The truth's cruel but I've got to say it. It's Natalie Demaine he wants. How do you think he'd feel if he had to marry you instead? He's a gentleman, right enough. Maybe he wouldn't show it. But there's no doubt he'd resent what he'd had to do and you'd feel it, even if the bairn didn't. We'll manage without any of them, never you fear,' she went on to say. 'Trust me, I'll help you.'

And she had. They had left Ellermere and moved to Manchester where Aunt Lily had obtained the position of housekeeper to Philip Ackroyd. Even with her Aunt Lily's support it had been a hard decision to make but through the years she had come to believe that it was the correct one. Only now after seeing Matt again did she begin to wonder. What would Tim do if he ever discovered that Matt Seymour was his father? What would he think of her for hiding the truth from him? Would he hate her for what she had done? Her life ten years ago had been in a disastrous muddle. Had she made it worse by not confiding in the Seymours? She doubted if she would ever know. It was probably a doubt she would have to live with for the rest of her life.

She sighed faintly, shaking her head. Tim was trudging up the slope towards her and she forced the disturbing thoughts out of her brain, almost as if she was afraid he would see them written on her face.

'Are you nearly finished, Mum?' he groaned, flopping on to the waterproof at her side. 'I'm tired.' He leaned forward, dark hair falling over his face as he peered over her shoulder to look at her sketch.

She saw his face and laughed ruefully. 'It will never make the Royal Academy will it? Never mind, it's been a pleasant break coming up here. I shall get back to work tomorrow with renewed enthusiasm.'

Tim pulled a face. 'School for me I suppose?'

'Definitely school for you, my lad,' Helen replied firmly, hiding a smile. 'Now get up and let me pack the rucksack, there's a love.'

Tim looked gloomy for a moment but brightened when a jay flew across the clearing in front of him and he rushed across the snow to take a closer look. Helen smiled to herself as she packed the picnic things into the bag. He would soon get over his momentary upset. He never actually complained when the time for school arrived. She was lucky; he never had, not even when he was very small. It was the thought that seemed daunting, particularly after a couple of unexpected days' holiday.

They walked down through the trees together, their breath cloudy in the still, cold air. The sun was already sinking. Daylight faded rapidly at this time of year and it was colder than ever now. Helen's fingers were freezing, even though her woollen mittens. Tim was very quiet. She guessed he was tired. She felt very weary herself, last night's lack of sleep catching up with her, she realised.

The sun was setting in a fierce, golden ball behind the trees when they finally came in sight of the cottage. A farm dog barked somewhere, but even the birds were silent now. Helen could see the smoke curling lazily from the chimney and she thought of the warm fire and the cosy little room with pleasure. It might be small and a little shabby but she had made it comfortable with her favourite books and pictures and the cheerful curtains at the windows.

'Race you!' Tim yelled suddenly, his voice piercing her abstraction. And as she watched he began to career down the hill at top speed, legs and arms flying in all directions. 'Last one home does the washing up after tea,' he shouted, his cheeks almost as red as his scarlet jacket.

Helen's smile was rueful as she walked along behind him. He was half running, half sliding down the hillside now, his legs and the bottom half of his anorak completely covered in snow but as she watched he slithered to a halt and she could see his broad grin from where she was standing. The snowball he threw was remarkably accurate, spluttering on Helen's shoulder, spraying her face with moisture.

She laughed, brushing the snow away with one hand and then she began to run, bending to scoop a handful of snow, pressing it into a firm, round ball and throwing it at Tim's rapidly retreating back. He was shouting aloud now, a happy, excited sound piercing the stillness of the late afternoon and although Helen kept up a stream of soft missiles she didn't manage to hit him once. He dodged this way and that, panting and laughing. Coming to a sudden halt as he rounded the path in front of the house. Helen flew round the corner after him, snowball at the ready.

'I've got you now, Tim Delaney,' she yelled and then she stopped just as abruptly as her son had done, the laughter draining out of her vivid face, an expression of horrified amazement frozen in its place.

CHAPTER FOUR

MATT SEYMOUR had just strolled out from under the porch, tall and dark, his hands thrust deep into the pockets of his sheepskin, and Helen knew it was already too late to send Tim away. What could she say to him anyway? 'Go and wait in the trees until Mr Seymour has gone.' He would think she was crazy. In any event he was already on his way up the garden path, the gate swinging wildly behind him. Matt had been watching her, his eyes narrowed disturbingly on her face, but even as Helen watched his gaze swivelled, to look long and hard at her son, his body stiffening, his hands coming slowly out of his pockets as Tim got closer to him.

Helen followed Tim up the path in a daze. She knew that unconsciously she had been expecting something like this to happen ever since Matt turned up on her doorstep yesterday evening, but worrying that it was going to happen didn't mean that she was armoured against it now it had. Matt still hadn't spoken. He was simply staring at Tim like a man in a state of shock. She seemed to be good at doing that to him, Helen reflected wryly and from the expression on his face he didn't appreciate it.

Helen had reached him now, her arm sliding over Tim's shoulders in an instinctively protective gesture. Matt removed his gaze from her son with an obvious effort, turning those dark brown eyes on her. He spoke now, still watching her, his eyes saying something completely at odds with the words he uttered.

'My mother was worried about you,' he stated flatly. 'She insisted that I come back and bring you some food . . . milk, bread and so on.' He indicated two laden bags on the floor of the porch. 'She seems to think you're on the point of starving to death.'

'It's very kind of her.' Helen's lips felt frozen and it wasn't only the icy wind that was affecting them. She looked at Tim. What must he be thinking? He was gazing from one to the other of them, obviously sensing that something was wrong, trying to read their faces but still not able to pin the problem down. Helen prayed silently that Matt would just go and leave them alone, but one look at his face told her she was praying for a lost cause.

'I want to talk to you.' Matt's eyes were as cold as the glittering landscape as he stared at Helen and she bit her lip glancing at Tim and back again.

'I'm not sure that we have anything to talk about, Mr Seymour,' she murmured huskily.

He bent forward, his dark head very close to hers. 'I can assure you that we have, Mrs Delaney.' His voice was as coldly formal as Helen's had been but her sensitive ears detected the hidden threat and his next words merely confirmed her fears.

'We can either have our little discussion right here and now or we can talk privately later. Which would you prefer?'

He was blackmailing her, Helen realised in rising panic. He guessed that Tim knew nothing and it was either do as he said or he would tell her son everything that he suspected. She knew she had lost the battle before she had even started fighting. There was no way she could counter that silent threat.

'We'll go inside,' she muttered huskily, searching her anorak pockets for the key.

'You haven't introduced me to your son yet, Mrs Delaney. I would like to meet him.' Matt's deep voice interrupted her search and she raised her head, her blue eyes stormy. He had hated the way she spoke to him earlier today and now he had a weapon he could use against her he was really turning the screw. She took a deep breath, her eyes on Tim's bent head. He was standing quietly, very pale. Helen recognised that look. He realised there was something drastically wrong. He was frightened, but too proud to show it and Helen hated Matt Seymour all over again for what he was doing to her son.

'Tim, this is Mr Seymour. I told you about him if you remember,' she murmured, keeping her voice as calm and unworried as she could make it.

Tim raised his head at last, the small, tentative hand he held out politely enveloped in Matt's firm handshake. 'Hello, Tim, it's nice to meet you.' Matt's voice had softened. There was even a faint smile curving his hard mouth and Tim responded to the fleeting warmth.

He smiled back. 'It's nice to meet you, sir. Mum said that your little girl liked my rabbits.'

Matt actually laughed now, pulling a face, his voice very deep and warm. 'So she did, but I'm afraid my own feelings towards them aren't quite so friendly. She's done nothing but talk about rabbits since she arrived home. She's even beginning to irritate her grandmother and believe me that takes some doing.'

Tim was grinning. 'They're really quite easy to look after once you've built them a nice, warm cage,' he said.

'Don't you start, Tim Delaney, or it will definitely be rabbit stew for supper.'

Helen had found the key at last and she pushed between them crossly. Tim was gazing up at Matt, smiling shyly. This was turning into a mutual admiration society where they were concerned and she felt a primitive urge to kick Matt's shins as she walked past him. He only had to turn on the Seymour charm and everyone was eating out of his hand. Well not her! She pushed the key into the lock with vicious emphasis, overwhelmingly conscious of Matt's tall, silent figure at her side. As usual the lock stuck and she struggled with it, turning it savagely, muttering under her breath. It didn't help when Matt reached out from behind her, his cool hand closing around her suddenly nerveless fingers.

'Let me try,' he murmured. And of course the key turned instantly. He stepped to one side, a faintly mocking hand gesturing for Helen to enter. She marched past him, her head high. Damn Matt Seymour! Damn him for walking back into her life like this and damn him for the way he made her feel. The touch of his fingers on her hand had been electric, a tiny quiver of excitement shooting along her veins.

She hung her coat behind the door and stalked over to the fire with restrained fury. She knew Matt was still lounging in the open doorway. She could feel his eyes on her back but she didn't turn around. Matt Seymour had invited himself. She was damned if she was going to play the eager hostess into the bargain. She stabbed at the logs with the poker now, tiny, glowing sparks flying in all directions as she heard Tim asking if he could take Matt's coat.

'I thought we could go and look at those rabbits first,' said Matt.

'That'd be great.' Tim was enthusiastic. 'You don't mind do you, Mum?' he asked.

Helen raised her head reluctantly, smoothing the tangled blonde curls away from her flushed cheeks.

'No, I don't mind,' she said. But she did, of course. She resented the ease with which Matt had charmed her son. Tim was hers! She didn't want Matt interfering in their lives. She said none of this but Tim sensed something of her attitude and simply stood without moving, his expression uncertain.

'Go on, love, if you're going.' Helen knew her tone was sharp but it was impossible to control it. Tim's face fell but after another faintly anxious look in his mother's direction he went out closely followed by Matt. Helen sighed when the door had closed behind them, sagging on to the sofa, her expression grim. Poor Tim, she had agreed to speak to Matt to prevent him discovering some painful truths and now she was upsetting him herself. She very rarely lost her temper with him these days. He must be totally confused. But then so was she and the worried lines on her brow deepened as she rose to her feet to fetch matches from the kitchen. She reached up to light the gas lamps one by one, her graceful figure bathed in a gentle, golden glow as each small jet of gas burst into flame.

Just what was Matt thinking at this moment? she wondered anxiously. Had the events of the evening Tim was conceived come rushing back into his brain in blinding technicolour the minute he had seen her son? Helen sighed again realising that such speculation was useless. She didn't have a clue what Matt Seymour was thinking. But no doubt he would tell her himself in his own good time.

That in itself was a far from reassuring thought and her gaze was still abstracted as she finished the lamps and began to unpack the rucksack, rinsing out the vacuum flask in the small, stone sink. The evening was going to be difficult, there was no doubt about that, but for Tim's sake she would have to try and keep her temper. She had upset him once tonight. That was enough.

She finished the washing up and moved into the porch to hang up the rucksack, seeing Matt's laden carrier bags on the floor at her feet. They were heavy, and she soon realised why when she lugged them back into the kitchen. They were crammed full of goodies. Not only milk and bread, but delicious home made rolls, a small joint of beef, fresh vegetables, lamb chops, freshly baked scones and a yummy chocolate cake.

Lady Bountiful, Helen thought, her lip curling slightly but then she shook her head and sighed, angry with herself for her momentary bitterness. Mrs Seymour was grateful to her for looking after Katy and this was her way of showing it. She would have done the same herself if someone had helped Tim. She bustled around unpacking the bags, carrying the vegetables over to the sink to peel, refusing to worry about Matt, concentrating instead on preparing the evening meal. And when Tim and Matt came back into the house there was a delicious smell of grilling chops coming from the cooker. The table was set for three, with the chocolate cake as a magnificent centrepiece and Helen's smile was deliberately bright as she walked out of the kitchen wiping her hands on a small towel.

'Hello, you two. I was beginning to worry. I wondered whether the rabbits had turned carnivorous and eaten you instead of the cabbage leaves.'

Tim giggled. Clearly he had had an enjoyable time with Matt and forgotten Helen's previous bad temper. His face was flushed, his eyes bright. 'I was explaining to Mr Seymour how to build a rabbit hutch,' he said. 'But he thinks he'll have it built in the village instead.' He was still smiling and Matt flicked his cheek with a gentle finger.

'Don't laugh, brat, or I shall have to think of a fitting punishment.'

Helen deliberately hadn't looked at Matt when he came through the door but she did so now. He was smiling down at her son, one hand resting lightly on his shoulder and for a brief moment she had to turn away, hot, angry words blocking her throat. Leave him alone! She wanted to cry. You have no right to touch him. One brief, physical act that meant nothing to you doesn't make you a father. But she knew that for Tim's sake she could say none of these things. She took a deep breath, forcing a smile to her lips, making herself look at Matt again.

'Will you stay for dinner, Mr Seymour? Your mother packed enough food to feed an army.'

He faced her over Tim's head, his eyes narrowed, thick lashes lowered, watching her intently from under them as though trying to read what was behind her smile. Helen's face didn't alter but she couldn't prevent her expressive blue eyes from sending a silent challenge. For Tim's sake she would be pleasant but when she and Matt were alone she would tell him frankly to keep out of their lives. She had managed without his help for the last ten years. She would continue to do so.

Matt accepted her invitation, disappearing with Tim to his bedroom to look at his photographs whilst Helen put the finishing touches to the meal. Like Helen he seemed to have decided that for Tim's sake there ought to be a temporary truce between them. Dinner was a pleasant meal and Helen sat at the table surreptitiously watching Matt. He was lounging back in his seat, a lazy, relaxed warmth in the smile he was giving her son. He had once looked at her with that very same expression, Helen realised with a pang. She had always been a child to be humoured in his eyes. Even when others had seen she was a woman, he had continued to treat her with the same blend of teasing indulgence he reserved for the children of his acquaintance. It didn't improve her mood when she switched her gaze to her son's face. His cheeks were flushed with excitement and he was staring at Matt with all the unthinking adoration of childhood.

Helen's heart sank still further as she listened. Apparently Matt had recently developed an interest in photography himself which on its own would have been enough to endear him to Tim, but there was more.

'Mr Seymour says he'll take me into Carlisle some day. There's a super camera shop in the town that sells lots of second-hand equipment.'

Like hell he will, Helen thought angrily but she only said, sweetly, 'That's very kind of him, Tim.'

Matt was watching her again. She knew he had caught sight of the hidden barb in her tones even if Tim hadn't. 'I'll just do the washing up and then I think it's time you went to bed,' she told her son. 'School tomorrow, you ought to have an early night.'

'Oh, Mum!'

Helen was already busy stacking plates. 'Definitely an early night,' she insisted, a smile softening her words. Whatever Matt was going to say to her she wanted him to get it over with and he couldn't do that until Tim was safely upstairs. She carried the plates into the kitchen, piling them into the bowl. She realised that Matt had followed her and kept her eyes firmly on the water running into the sink.

'Where would you like this putting?' he murmured quietly from behind her back.

'Anywhere will do.' Helen's tones were sharp and she didn't turn around. The pleasant manner had been for

Tim's sake. Matt needn't think he was welcome in her house because it just wasn't true.

'Don't tempt me, Helen,' he said and something in the deep tones made her head swivel round, her eyes wide. He was balancing what remained of the chocolate cake on one hand and he was smiling wickedly at her, his dark brows raised. Without really thinking she smiled back, her eyes meeting his in a moment of shared amusement.

'Be careful with that,' she murmured, still smiling. 'It was too delicious to waste.' And then she turned back to the sink, annoyed with herself for her momentary weakness. Matt's charm was as deadly as a rattlesnake bite. He had bowled Tim over without any trouble but she ought to have more sense than to fall for it. The dishes were soon washed and put away. Both Matt and Tim had taken a tea towel from the drawer and lent a helping hand. Thankfully Helen didn't need to talk. She just plunged the dishes into the hot, soapy water, turning them upside down on the wooden draining board when they were clean, listening as her son poured out his entire life story into Matt's interested ears. And all the time she could feel Matt watching her, but she didn't turn around. Let him pump Tim all he liked. He wouldn't discover anything that she didn't want him to hear.

'Don't you find it lonely at Fell Cottage, Tim?' Matt was asking now.

'Oh, no, it's great.' There was no doubting the enthusiasm of Tim's reply. 'It's not lonely anyway. Mr and Mrs Williams live next door and they've got lots of grandchildren who are always visiting. And in summer Uncle Phil usually comes to stay. We have a fantastic time then. He's a painter friend of Mum's and he knows everything there is to know about animals and birds.

He stayed for months last summer. He hired a car and we went all over the Lake District. He took me camping to Ullswater so Mum could finish her commission and then we all drove to Newcastle and sailed in the ferry to Norway. We were there for a whole month.'

These candid revelations all came out in an excited rush. Tim thought Philip Ackroyd was heaven's gift to small boys and he didn't care who knew it. But Helen had watched Matt secretly while Tim was talking and one look at that cynically smiling mouth had told her immediately what he was thinking. Well let him think it! She wasn't about to launch into long explanations for Matt Seymour's benefit. Even though he was over sixty Philip Ackroyd was her dearest friend and she had no intention of apologising for that friendship to anyone.

She slammed the last of the cups down on to the draining board, emptying water out of the plastic bowl so that it gurgled noisily down the sink. 'That's finished, thank you both.' She smiled, avoiding Matt's eyes. 'Would you like to sit in the other room and I'll make some coffee. It's much pleasanter drinking it around the fire.'

The talk over the coffee cups was desultory. They were all tired. Tim's head was nodding although he was struggling valiantly to keep his eyes open and Helen could have fallen asleep in her chair, she felt so weary. A combination of fresh air and exercise and lack of sleep last night, plus the emotional shocks the last twenty-four hours had thrown at her, had completely worn her out. Even Matt looked half asleep, his head thrown back, those slumbrous brown eyes half closed, his long limbs thrust out towards the blazing fire. On the surface it was a cosy, domestic scene, the warm room, the firelight reflecting on their drowsy faces. But it was a bit like reading one of Shakespeare's plays,

Helen reflected wearily. There were layers of meaning hidden from the casual observer. You had to look very closely before you could really begin to understand the intricacies of the situation. And even then motives and meanings were difficult to unravel.

Tim yawned suddenly, his hand rising automatically to cover his mouth and Helen rose to her feet, glad to be distracted from her thoughts. 'Bedtime, Tim,' she said.

Tim sighed, 'Oh, Mum.' But it was a weak protest. He was very tired and he washed quickly as Helen prepared a hot water bottle and slipped it into his bed. When she came back downstairs he was already saying good night to Matt, very tall and straight in his pyjamas and thick woollen dressing gown.

'You'll tell Katy she can come and look at my rabbits any time, won't you?' he was saying shyly.

Matt was smiling down at Tim, his eyes a very warm, velvety brown. 'Don't worry, Tim. I doubt whether I shall be able to keep her away. As I said, you and your rabbits are her sole topic of conversation at the moment.'

Tim climbed the stairs at last, quite happily and Helen followed him. Now the tête-à-tête with Matt was imminent she was not feeling quite so eager to embark on it. She sat on the edge of Tim's bed smiling down at him, his dark hair and bright eyes the only thing she could see as he snuggled down out of the cold. It had been a strange sensation watching them both together this evening, father and son . . . She hadn't realised just how alike they were until then. Of course her memories of Matt had faded over the years, hardened by her own bitter experience. She had forgotten how charming his smile could be. She had forgotten the caressing warmth of those dark eyes. She had forgotten his kindness, his

sense of humour. She hadn't wanted to remember, she
didn't want to remember now.

Helen's thoughts were in turmoil but she didn't allow
it to show on her face as she bent to kiss her son's
cheek, laughing as he tried to squirm out of range of
her lips. He was at the age when kissing was taboo but
he didn't really object when Helen tried to sneak one. It
had become a game between them. One that he didn't
mind losing.

'Got you that time,' she said with a grin and she was
still smiling when she walked down the stairs but her
mouth stiffened, her nerve endings thrumming with
awareness as she saw Matt studying her from his seat
on the sofa. He was still lounging in the same position
but now Helen got the feeling that his mood of
indolence was a façade for her benefit. Underneath all
that languid elegance he was as taut as a coiled spring.
Any minute he was going to let fly and she would be
lucky not to get caught in the backlash.

It was unnerving having to walk across the room in
front of those dark, assessing eyes. It would have helped
if she'd known what he was thinking but his face was
carefully blank. She was tempted to take a seat on the
sofa next to him, just to prove that he couldn't
intimidate her but at the last moment her courage failed
and she subsided on to the chair opposite instead. Matt
moved then, leaning forward in his seat, drawing her
eyes towards him.

'Tell me,' he said. 'Is this Uncle Phil that Tim talks
about, your lover?'

The question was so unexpected that Helen simply
stared at him for a moment, her jaw dropped. 'Mind
your own business,' she spluttered angrily when she had
finally caught her breath. The nerve of the man! Who
did he think he was?

'Perhaps I think it is my business,' he told her softly.

'Well, you can just think again.' Helen was really angry now, her blue eyes flashing. 'What I choose to do is my own concern and no one else's. If I want to take one lover or half a dozen, I will do so.'

'Delightful!' His firm lips curled into a faintly sardonic smile. 'What a charming lifestyle you must have.'

Helen glared at him, her face very flushed. 'I hardly think that you're in a position to criticise. Your own approach this morning wasn't exactly subtle, was it? You really thought you'd landed on your feet last night, didn't you? I could see precisely what you were thinking. Little Helen Morley . . . a divorced woman, living on her own. You thought I was a ripe plum ready for picking. Well, you were mistaken,' Helen cried, her breast heaving angrily.

Matt stared back, his expression furious. 'You're a sharp-tongued little shrew, Helen Delaney.'

'I can't help it if you don't like the truth.'

'Your over-active imaginings bear no relation to the truth,' he snarled.

'Tell that to the marines!'

Matt's colour darkened to a deep, angry red. 'To think, at one time I believed that you were a sweet, innocent little angel.'

Helen forced a tight, angry smile. 'I still am! You just haven't discovered the real me, Mr Seymour.'

'Steven did, I suppose,' he muttered, his expression still grim.

Helen shook her head. 'I don't know what you're talking about.'

He laughed harshly. 'Oh come on, Helen, I've got eyes. Tim is the spitting image of Steven at that age. You'd been going around with my brother for months before you left Ellermere. Everyone knew you adored him. We wondered why you and your aunt left in such a tearing hurry and now we know, don't we.'

Helen stared at him wide-eyed for a moment and then she began to laugh, her mouth open, her head thrown back in a kind of hysterical amusement. Perhaps she ought to have expected him to come to that conclusion, but foolishly it had never entered her head. He was still watching her angrily and she caught her breath. 'Tim is not Steven's son!'

'Don't give me that! Tim's a Seymour down to his fingertips.'

Helen had sobered completely now. 'Poor Tim,' she murmured, her expression deliberately mocking, and he sighed.

'I warn you, Helen. You're really asking for trouble.'

Helen smiled again, that same mocking curve of her soft lips. 'And you're going to give it to me, I suppose,' she murmured sweetly.

He shook his head. 'Don't tempt me. The urge to shake you is almost overwhelming,' he warned, and Helen felt a tiny shiver of fear and excitement at the expression in his eyes. But still she couldn't prevent herself from taunting him further.

'In fact, the perfect gentleman,' she mocked.

For a moment she thought he was going to carry out his threat but then he took a long, steadying breath, relaxing deliberately, his head thrown back against the sofa cushions so that Helen's eyes were drawn, as if by a magnet, to the smooth, muscular length of his tanned throat beneath the open neck of his shirt. He turned his head, running a hand over his eyes. 'This is getting us nowhere,' he sighed. 'I don't usually lose my temper so easily.'

'And you think I do,' Helen retorted huskily.

He sighed again after she had spoken, giving her a very intent stare. Helen found his dark eyes extremely disturbing. It was almost as though he could read her mind, and at that moment her thoughts were hardly suitable for public consumption. 'This is an emotional subject. It's difficult to discuss it calmly, I do realise that,' he said.

Helen shook her head. 'I don't agree with you. You have jumped to conclusions about Tim and they simply aren't the correct ones.' Secretly, now that the first shock had passed, she was intensely relieved that Matt believed Steven to be Tim's father. She had every intention of continuing to deny it, of course and she could do so with a clear conscience, knowing that in all probability he wouldn't believe her.

'Don't be a fool, Helen,' Matt was saying now. 'I'm not trying to pass judgment when I say that Steven is Tim's father.'

'That's big of you!'

He ignored that comment, only the tightening of his jaw telling her that he had heard it. 'I want to help you, can't you understand that? I want to help both of you. God knows why you didn't come to us when you first realised you were pregnant.'

'Maybe because it had nothing to do with you. Tim is my son. He doesn't belong to Steven, or any other member of the Seymour family. His name is Timothy Delaney . . .'

'Like hell!' Matt's face expressed his feelings very clearly. 'Maybe he's not officially called Seymour, but he damned well ought to be.'

'He's Tim Delaney,' Helen muttered stubbornly.

'You're saying he's your husband's son, is that it?'

'I'm not saying anything. I don't have to explain myself to you.'

'I've told you, I only want to help,' Matt sighed frustratedly. 'Steven got you into this mess and I intend to do what I can to get you out.' His strong-boned face looked aggressively determined, his mouth tight, his jaw out-thrust and Helen shook her head fiercely, firelight catching the soft curls feathering across her forehead.

'What do I have to say to convince you? I don't want your help! I don't need your help!' She was on her feet and had walked across the room in short, angry strides, taking Matt's coat down from the hook behind the door. He had turned and was watching her as she held the sheepskin out towards him. 'We have nothing more to discuss, Mr Seymour. I realise that you can cause difficulties in my life by telling Tim what you suspect but somehow I don't think that you will do that.'

He shook his head. 'I don't know what game you're playing, Helen. I don't know why you're behaving like this . . .'

'I'm not playing any game,' she told him tautly. 'I didn't ask to see you. I certainly didn't intend to meet you again. You came into my life by accident and now I simply want you to leave it again, as quickly as possible. Stay away from both Tim and myself. At the risk of being boringly repetitive, let me say again, we don't need you! We don't want you!'

'I'll go for now,' he stated abruptly. He was standing by the door, the tense curve of his body posing a silent threat. 'You're right about one thing. I don't want to upset Tim. But I'll be back,' he promised. 'And then I'll get the truth out of you if I have to shake you to do it.'

And that was no empty threat, Helen decided with a shiver as she watched his angry figure striding through the snow towards the road. The Seymours were a possessive race. Generations of being lords of all they surveyed had bred that into them and Matt Seymour was no different in that respect. He had decided that Tim had Seymour blood in his veins and Helen was afraid that he wouldn't rest until he had dragged them both back into his family's orbit. Not because he cared anything for them but simply because he had some misguided notion they were a family responsibility.

CHAPTER FIVE

Two weeks later Helen was still waiting for Matt's threatened return. At first she had been worried every time she went back to the cottage, half expecting to see his tall figure emerging from the porch as she approached, but finally she had realised that he must have decided to leave them alone as she had demanded. She was deeply relieved, of course, although she was still finding it difficult to relax. She couldn't forget his earlier visits quite so easily and even Tim had noticed her self-absorption.

'Don't worry, love, I'm fine,' she reassured him when he asked her what was wrong. 'Painting those butterflies is getting me down, that's all.'

And that was true enough, Helen reflected now as she trudged up the path from the bus stop, the laden shopping bags turning her fingers blue. Her latest commission was a small set of butterfly illustrations for a private collector. Her agent had sent her the tropical specimens a few days ago and she shuddered every time she had to look at them. They were beautiful but they made her feel sick, their fragile wings stretched, jewel bright behind glass, cruelly pinned to a mount. When she painted insects or animals she liked to study them in their natural habitat, although that hadn't been a practical proposition in this instance, she conceded honestly—unless her agent had suffered a momentary brainstorm and offered to fly her out to the Seychelles for a couple of weeks.

If only! Helen thought with a wry grimace, as she

dumped her heavy bags in the snow and collapsed weakly back against a tree to catch her breath. That was exactly what she needed. A holiday, a change of scene and new faces around her. It had been a severe winter and right now she was suffering from the effects. But a holiday was out of the question and her expression was wry as she picked up her bags reluctantly and began to move up the slope again. The snow was still thick around the cottage and although the sun was shining, the wind was icy, blowing straight off the top of the fells. The first thing Helen did when she got into the house was build up the fire, putting on some smaller pieces of wood to encourage the blaze.

She had been longer than she expected in the village. It was one of those days when everyone she met wanted to talk and without snubbing them unforgivably she had no choice but to stand and listen as though she had all the time in the world. They didn't understand, of course, Helen reflected as she unpacked her bags in the kitchen, putting the eggs and butter she had bought into the fridge, piling vegetables into the scarlet rack beside the sink. They knew she was an artist and they equated that with a life of leisure. They didn't realise that she had to work to a timetable like everyone else.

She turned on a gas ring and lit it, putting the kettle over the heat. She was still frozen and she knew she wouldn't be able to work until some warmth had crept back into her fingers. Hopefully a cup of coffee would help. She was quite well on with the butterfly illustrations and she was eager to complete them. Once they were on their way to her agent she was determined to spend some time in the open air painting the things she wanted to paint. The owner of the craft shop in Ambleside who sold her water-colours was already begging for more and it would be no hardship to oblige him.

She drank her coffee and began to paint at last, dragging the dining table in front of the window to get full benefit of the morning light. It was a beautiful, crisp, sunny day again and she stared outside regretfully for a moment before turning her back deliberately, concentrating instead on the fragile, brightly coloured wings of the tropical butterfly. She took a break at one, walking into the kitchen flexing her aching shoulders, her face drawn and weary. It was tiring doing such intricate work for long periods. Her spine ached and there was the beginning of a throb behind her eyes which promised a full scale headache later on in the day if she wasn't careful.

The kettle boiled and she made some more coffee, cutting two slices of bread and butter, filling them with cheese. She ate in front of the fire, flicking through a women's magazine she had bought in the village, her mind only partly occupied by the glossy pages. She could hear Mr Williams outside with one of his grandchildren and when she had finished eating she wandered over to the window to watch them. The little girl was shrieking excitedly as she pelted her grandfather with snowballs. They were wildly off course but Susie didn't seem to mind; she still kept throwing them as Fred Williams' lanky figure darted this way and that, pretending to dodge every one.

She was very lucky having such delightful neighbours, Helen reflected, smiling to herself as Mr Williams pretended to fall over, and landed in a snow drift, his mouth open in a circle of shocked surprise. They had taken Tim to their hearts, welcoming him into their house and family as though he was a dearly loved grandchild instead of a near stranger and Helen knew she would never be able to thank them enough for their kindness.

Susie was still shrieking excitedly when Helen eventually turned away from the window. She would have liked to go out and join them but she knew she had to resist temptation. She sat down and picked up her paint brush, getting down to work almost immediately, carefully painting delicate strokes of royal blue, ignoring the shouts and laughter from outside. When the knock came at the porch door a couple of hours later she was ready for another break. She stood up, stretching tiredly. That would be Mrs Williams, Helen realised. She had promised to pay her rates bill when she took Tim to school tomorrow. Mrs Williams would be bringing the money.

She ran a hand through her hair as she walked towards the door, the action doing little to straighten the tangled curls. She opened the door, smiling.

'I was going to come round . . .' The words slowly trailed away into silence. Maybe she ought to have expected Matt Seymour, but she hadn't. She stared at him for a moment, the smile freezing on her lips. He didn't seem to have much to say for himself either. He simply stared back at her, his narrowed eyes intent on her slim figure in the tight jeans and scarlet sweater.

Helen could feel her colour rising, staining her cheeks a vivid red. 'Just what do I have to say to convince you that you aren't welcome here?' she demanded angrily. 'Just go away and stay away, Mr Seymour!'

'I want to talk to you, Helen,' he said.

'Get lost!' she cried and began to shut the door, but somehow his foot was in the way and she didn't quite dare to slam it in case she hurt him in the process. 'And take your foot out of the door or I'll scream. Mr and Mrs Williams are at home today. They'd be bound to hear.'

Matt's expression was almost smug, his brown eyes

gleaming mockingly into hers. 'Yes, I've just seen them. They were walking down into the village with one of their grandchildren as I was driving up the hill.'

Helen exhaled sharply. Just my luck, she thought and at that moment Matt gave a swift push, propelling Helen helplessly back into the room. Matt followed her in, slamming the door behind him, his dark, quilted skiing jacket making him look bigger and more aggressively formidable than ever. Helen threw back her head, blonde curls tossing, her blue eyes blazing angrily.

'You really have a nerve, don't you?' she snapped.

'I told you, I want to talk to you.'

Matt rocked back on his heels, hands in his jacket pocket, watching her revealing expression with guarded eyes.

'And if you want something, you just reach out and take it, whatever anyone else says, is that right?' Helen retorted angrily.

'Don't be a fool,' he sighed. 'I've told you before, I'm here because I'm trying to help you and for no other reason.'

Helen's hands were clenched fists at her sides. 'And I've told you I don't want your help. Just what do I have to say to convince you?'

'You never will convince me. Just as you will never persuade me that Tim is not Steven's son,' he shot back at once, his mouth a hard, determined line.

'Oh you ...' Helen stared at him with frustrated, angry eyes and then she stalked over to the fireplace, leaning against it, turning her back on him deliberately, her blonde head propped on one shaking hand. 'Just say what you have to say and go,' she told him fiercely, the words muffled by her bent head. 'Contrary to popular opinion an artist's life is not one continual holiday and I do have work to do before I collect Tim.'

'I've got the car. I'll collect the boy from school,' he told her brusquely.

Helen's head did swing round at that. 'Like hell you will! Keep away from my son,' she snarled.

He ignored her angry response, his face as calmly determined as before. 'I'm taking you both back to Ellermere for the evening. My mother wants to see you again . . . and to meet Tim. I would have come before now but I had to go to France on business.'

Helen knew that her colour had risen again. What had he told his mother about Tim? Had he told Mrs Seymour that Tim was Steven's son? Of course he must have done. She couldn't imagine that Madeline Seymour would have expressed a wish to see her again otherwise. But she wasn't going. No way! She had no intention of getting involved with the Seymour family again.

'You could have saved yourself the trouble today,' she muttered now, her flush fading rapidly, leaving her pale, her expression as determined as Matt Seymour's own. 'Neither Tim nor I are coming with you. It was kind of your mother to invite us but it wasn't necessary.'

'Not even to see her own grandson?'

'Tim is nothing to do with you or any other member of your family. He's my son. He's Tim Delaney.' Helen shot the words at him, feeling as though she was banging her head against a brick wall and even now Matt was visibly unmoved by her denials.

'Like hell he is!' he snapped, moving very quickly so that almost before Helen knew it he was standing directly in front of her, staring down into her eyes. 'I don't know whether you have ever been married as you say, and believe me, I don't really care. You could have had half a dozen husbands but none of them would be

Tim's father and there's no way you can convince me otherwise.'

Helen's chin jutted, her soft mouth set in a stubborn line. 'Tim is a Delaney!'

'For God's sake, Helen!' He reached out and gripped her shoulders. 'Why must you be such a little fool? I don't want to take Tim away from you, if that's what you think and I'm darned sure Steven wouldn't want to do so either. I admire the way you've managed on your own over the last few years. I just want to make things easier for you, for both of you.' His voice was changing, softening, deepening as his fingers tightened on the soft flesh of her shoulders. 'I don't want to hurt you, Helen,' he murmured. 'I don't want us to be enemies. We were good friends once. Couldn't we be friends again?'

Taken off guard by his sudden change of mood Helen raised her eyes and stared up at him and when he lowered his head and touched her lips gently with his own she simply stood there for a moment, rooted to the spot, so surprised by his unexpected action that not only didn't she struggle, but her lips parted automatically in shock. His kiss deepened immediately, his arms tightening, sliding around her waist, drawing her closer so that she could feel every muscular inch of his lean, hard body. His lips were still moving with seductive warmth over her own. She was trembling, she realised, her heart hammering wildly in her breast and for one brief, devastating moment she was tempted to stay in his embrace, allow her arms to slide around his neck and kiss him back, thrust her fingers into his thick dark hair, press herself against him . . .

But it was only a momentary weakness. Common sense reasserted itself almost immediately and then she was fighting, pushing him away with all her strength, twisting her body out of his arms, her palms flat against his heaving chest. 'No!' she cried in a shaky voice. 'Let me go!' And he released her abruptly, stepping back, raking an unsteady hand through his dark hair, his lips twisted into a faint, rueful grimace of apology.

'Helen, I'm sorry. I didn't intend that to happen. Don't look at me like that, please,' he sighed.

She faced him, trembling so badly she could barely speak. 'I think you had better go,' she whispered.

He took a small step forward and Helen retreated instinctively before him. He stopped abruptly, shaking his head. 'It won't happen again, I promise you. It wasn't premeditated. I was angry and upset, what followed was just a natural progression.'

'And you think that makes it okay, I suppose.'

'Of course it doesn't, but for heaven's sake, it was only a kiss . . .'

He would have said more but Helen didn't give him the opportunity. 'I'm glad you realise that. Now, if you'll kindly leave.' She pointed to the door with a surprisingly steady hand. It seemed to be the only part of her that wasn't still trembling. Her legs felt like jellies and she was afraid they would give out on her at any moment and she wanted Matt to leave before that happened. His kiss had disturbed her more than she would have believed possible. It hadn't been a particularly long or intensely passionate encounter but the touch of his lips had started a chain reaction inside her and she was still suffering from the after effects.

Matt was walking across the room now, but he turned as he reached the door. 'I'm going, Helen, don't worry.' His mood had hardened under the lash of Helen's tongue and there was no hint of warmth in his voice as he added, 'I shall be back. In twenty minutes to be precise. After I've collected Tim from school. Don't worry, he is expecting me. My mother rang the

headmaster earlier today. She didn't want him to think
I was abducting your son.'

Helen was speechless for a moment, her eyes dazed
with shock at his high-handed tactics. 'You never give
up, do you, you bloody Seymours?' she cried.

But Matt just smiled, his eyes hard, ignoring her
words. 'Be ready when I get back, Helen. Otherwise I
shall take Tim to Ellermere on his own.'

He meant what he said, Helen realised, looking at the
implacable set of his hard features, and she couldn't
allow that to happen. She couldn't risk Tim getting
hurt.

He was still waiting by the half open door. 'Did you
hear me, Helen?' he asked and she nodded wearily.

'Don't worry, I shall be ready. But I don't know what
you expect to gain by this.'

'Would you believe, nothing?' he sighed. 'Because
that's the simple truth.' He looked across at Helen's
angry face for a moment as though tempted to say
more but then clearly thought better of it and without
another word, turned on his heel and left the cottage,
closing the door quietly behind himself.

Only then did Helen's composure break completely
and she raked shaking hands through her hair, her eyes
tight closed, her face twisted into an impotent paroxysm
of pain and fury. 'Stay out of my life, Matt Seymour!'
she cried, but even as her voice died away into silence
she knew her protests were useless. Matt had decided to
make himself responsible for Tim and herself and it
seemed that for the moment she was helpless and there
was nothing that she could do about it.

Half an hour later she was sitting in the Range Rover
deliberately not looking at the back of Matt Seymour's
dark head, directly in front of her. He had collected her
from the cottage as he had promised and although he

had tried to be friendly, she had ignored him, uncaring in that moment whether her behaviour upset her son. But unfortunately, as she was fast discovering, ignoring Matt Seymour in the flesh and putting him out of her mind were two totally different propositions. Her brain was an emotional minefield. Whichever way she turned, there he was in glorious technicolour, blocking her view. She couldn't even look through the misted glass at the gathering dusk without being reminded forcibly of him.

They were driving along the shores of Coniston Water at the moment and she could see the lake shimmering, deep and mysterious through the bare branches of the trees which bordered the road. She hadn't been back to this valley since leaving Ellermere ten years ago but it was still achingly familiar to her, every inch of it packed with memories. She had swum and sailed in the lake so many times and walked over every one of the fells behind it, tagging along after Matt and Steven.

Helen sighed now, a small sound which she stifled instantly. She had to stop thinking about the happy times they had shared in the past. She had to remember instead that Matt was a dangerously attractive man, a threat to her peace of mind, and she had to armour herself against him. Her reaction to his kiss ought surely to have taught her that. The temptation to kiss him back had been a disturbingly strong one and she still hadn't worked out quite how it had happened. She had been off balance, of course, his unexpected action taking her by surprise but that didn't completely explain her foolish reaction.

But then again, maybe the explanation was even more simple. She had fought shy of men for years, recognising that as a woman on her own with a small child she promised an easy target. Matt was the first man in years to have tried to get close to her, the first man for ages not to be discouraged by the cold, uninterested façade she presented. Helen knew that her cold manner was only a façade. She needed warmth and love as much as anyone else, it was just that she had buried that need and Matt's unexpected kiss had reawakened it.

Helen was relieved to have come to such a satisfactory conclusion and she relaxed back in her seat, feeling brave enough now to risk a brief glance to the front of the car where her son and Matt Seymour were sitting. Unfortunately it was a far from reassuring sight. Tim was chattering away to Matt as though he had known him all his life and Helen didn't need a crystal ball to recognise troubled waters ahead. Tim was a delightful boy, everyone said so, and until now she had had very few problems with him but she had an unpleasant feeling that her difficulties might just be beginning.

The way he looked at his father—the expression of adoration shining out of his eyes—frightened her. At the moment Matt was his hero. His unexpected arrival at the school gates had made her son blissfully happy. There were no problems on his horizon, no worries. Unfortunately Helen couldn't feel quite so sanguine about the future. Even the immediate present was enough to frighten her to death. They had already left the main road and were climbing the hill towards Ellermere House, the headlights of the Range Rover piercing the dark tunnel of trees ahead and reflecting on the deep piles of snow lying at either side of the road.

Soon they would be at the house and just what would happen then? she wondered. Exactly what had Matt told his mother about them? Had Mrs Seymour issued this invitation for their visit, as Matt said, or was the whole thing his idea? She wished she knew. And she shifted restlessly on her seat, leaning forward a little as Tim's tiny gasp of amazement made her realise that they had emerged from the shadow of the trees at last and Ellermere House lay in front of them.

Tim was staring as though he couldn't quite believe his eyes and Helen remembered that her own reactions had been very similar when she had first arrived with Aunt Lily. She had been just as awed as Tim by its size and the elegant lines of its stone façade. The house must look like a palace to him. And it was beautiful, she admitted to herself as the car slowly gentled to a halt in front of the main entrance. She had forgotten just how beautiful. Built of warm, golden stone, its frontage brightly illuminated by discreetly positioned spotlights, the same two stone lions guarded the entrance Helen saw with a faint smile.

Tim still hadn't spoken and she watched from beneath her lashes as Matt smiled down at him, clearly enjoying his admiration. The house had been in his family for generations. He was justifiably proud of his inheritance. Helen was still watching Tim and for the first time she saw the full significance of his paternity. Had her own actions been different ten years ago in all likelihood Tim would have been Matt's heir. It was a far from comfortable thought and one which she thankfully thrust to the back of her mind as the front door of the house flew open, welcome golden light spilling on to the porch illuminating the two figures framed in the doorway.

The smaller of the two was undoubtedly Katy, with Madeline Seymour standing next to her. Helen's mouth was suddenly dry, her heartbeats hammering away like sledgehammers in her breast. The snarling lions guarding the entrance were very appropriate she decided with a tiny grimace. She felt rather like Daniel must have done before he was thrown into the wild beast's den. She climbed out of the car, carefully not looking at Matt as he held the door open for her, climbing the steps towards the front entrance past the lions, Tim at her side, feeling almost as though she was in a dream.

This was one place to which she had never intended to return. She was a fool! She ought to have called Matt's bluff and refused to accompany him. Tim seemed to be having second thoughts now, as well. He was walking very close to her as though he needed the reassurance and she glanced down sensing his discomfort. He was holding himself very straight, his soft mouth set in a determined line and as she watched, he looked up, his eyes anxious. Maybe he'd sensed her own nervousness, Helen thought, and she forced a smile.

'Okay, love?' she murmured, trying to reassure him when she couldn't even reassure herself.

He smiled back bravely. 'Okay, Mum,' he replied.

But Helen knew he was scared. She also knew who was to blame for landing them in this awkward situation so that when Matt's hand curved around her elbow it seemed like the final indignity and she would have dragged her arm away except that she was overwhelmingly conscious of their silent audience—Mrs Seymour and Katy standing in the open doorway. And as though on cue Mrs Seymour stepped forward now, her slim figure very erect, the brown eyes, so like her son's, moving from Tim to Matt and back to Helen.

'You've arrived safely, we were beginning to worry.' Her cultured tones were strained and anxious as they stopped in front of her. Tim shrank even further into

Helen's side. He was very bright for nine years old and
even though he didn't understand the reasons, he was
picking up the tension in the atmosphere. He knew
there was something wrong. For a moment no one
spoke or moved, even Matt seemed at a loss for words.
It was Katy who broke the strained silence. She had
noticed nothing except that her father had brought Tim
to visit her as he had promised. She pulled her hand out
of her grandmother's restraining clasp and danced
across to them.

'Hello, Mrs Delaney.' She smiled sweetly at Helen
and then transferred her attention to Tim. 'I saw your
rabbits and gave them some cabbage leaves, did your
mummy tell you?' she asked, brown eyes sparkling.

'Yes, thanks.' Helen was proud of her son. His tones
were diffident but he was determined not to show his
nervousness in front of these strangers. 'It saved me a
job,' he added. 'I only had to give them some clean
water after that.'

Katy took his hand unselfconsciously. 'Come inside,
Tim. Daddy bought me a book all about rabbits. I want
to show it to you.' And as though his daughter's words
had pushed the correct button Matt too was galvanised
into speech.

'Yes, it's foolish standing around out here.' And his
hand on Helen's arm tightened as he began to urge
them all inside. 'And before you drag Tim off with you
I'd like him to meet your grandmother,' he said to his
daughter.

It was painful for Helen to watch the two of them
together. Matt's fingers gripping Tim's shoulder, his
eyes on the bent head so like his own. 'Mother, this is
Tim Delaney, the young man I've been telling you
about,' he said.

There was a silent message in his words and only Tim

and Katy were blissfully unaware of it. Tim's greeting
was polite, but nothing more. He saw no reason to be
especially interested in Matt's mother. He was more
interested in Katy, Helen realised and when Katy pulled
him along the corridor towards the stairs he went with
her quite cheerfully, throwing a half-sheepish, half
apologetic glance over his shoulder at Helen.

It was very quiet in the hall when they had gone. The
grandfather clock ticked in slow, regular rhythm and
the logs in the grate crackled, throwing out angry, red
sparks. Mrs Seymour was watching the two children
running along the corridor and Helen stared down at
the toes of her soft, leather boots, avoiding Matt's eyes.
This was horrible. Madeline Seymour didn't want her
here. It was as she had thought, the invitation was
really Matt's idea.

'Mother, you remember Helen.' Matt's tone was
brusque now, reminding Mrs Seymour of her responsibilities as a hostess.

She turned to Helen immediately, an unmistakably
warm, welcoming smile on her lips. She held out her
hands taking Helen's cold fingers in her own warm
clasp. 'It's been a long time, my dear,' she murmured,
leaning forward to kiss Helen's cheek. 'Welcome back
to Ellermere! Welcome home.'

CHAPTER SIX

THANKS to Madeline Seymour, Helen's first evening back at Ellermere was a much easier and far more comfortable occasion than she had expected. The house itself had altered very little; the whole effect still one of comfort and unpretentious elegance. The suite in the drawing room had been re-upholstered in a quiet shade of blue, she noticed as she walked in and sat down. There were new drapes at the window and one or two pieces of highly polished furniture which Helen didn't recognise. But the elegant, cream marble fireplace housed a blazing log fire as it had always done in winter and there were flowers in beautiful containers on every available surface, delicate freesias, yellow and white daffodils, pots of cineraria and pink cyclamen. Mr Seymour had always loved to see fresh flowers in the house and it was reassuring somehow to know that they had still kept on the tradition now he was dead.

It was Madeline Seymour's appearance which had startled Helen most. She had always had immaculately good taste in clothes and that at least hadn't changed. Her severely styled dark suit breathed Paris even to Helen's unsophisticated eyes and her own simple pleated skirt and cream woollen sweater seemed cheap and shapeless by contrast. But the expensive clothes couldn't alter the fact that Mrs Seymour had aged enormously since Helen had seen her last. Her beautiful dark hair was heavily streaked with grey, her face was gaunt and pale, dominated by the large, brown eyes with their fringe of thick, dark lashes which were now her only real claim to beauty. Matt said she had been ill and clearly it was true. Her husband's death must have affected her deeply, Helen reflected as they sat opposite each other on the blue velvet chairs, talking quietly. They had always been very close, and George Seymour had been such a powerful, vibrantly alive personality that his death must have left a huge, aching hole in Madeline Seymour's existence.

But Mrs Seymour's warmth and kindness were still the same as ever and once Matt had disappeared into his study Helen felt considerably more comfortable. Matt's mother was intensely interested in everything that had happened to Helen since leaving Ellermere and under the influence of her gently probing conversation Helen found herself relating far more of her life history than she had intended. And it didn't help to realise that at some point during the proceedings Matt had walked back into the room, but when she raised her eyes he was standing beside the tray of drinks, a glass of whisky in one hand, watching her.

Just how much had he heard? Helen wondered. Just how much of herself had she revealed to Madeline Seymour? Too much it seemed, because Mrs Seymour was watching her as well, her brown eyes filled with compassion.

'Oh Helen, my dear,' she murmured. 'You've had such a struggle. Why did you try to bear it on your own? Why didn't you come to us the moment you discovered you were pregnant? Surely you knew we would help you?'

'Tim is my son, my responsibility,' Helen said forcefully, trying to convince Madeline Seymour as she knew she would never convince Madeline's son.

Mrs Seymour sighed. 'But surely his father . . .' but then she stopped, leaning across to take Helen's fingers in her own, squeezing them gently. 'I'm sorry, my dear. Matt told me that this is something you simply don't want to discuss. I promised him I would be tactful, but seeing Tim I . . .' She paused a second time, shaking her head, her expression rueful. 'I think we had better change the subject immediately. I can see Matt frowning at me.'

'You're exaggerating as usual, Mother,' Matt responded smoothly, leaving his place by the sideboard, moving across to stand beside his mother's chair, glass of whisky in one hand. He looked across at Helen his expression bland, clearly determined not to make any waves this evening. 'What can I get you to drink?' he asked. 'Mrs Ellis tells me that dinner will be ready very shortly.'

In fact Helen had barely begun to sip the dry sherry he had poured for her before the housekeeper came to fetch them into the dining room. They were eating early as a concession to the children and both Tim and Katy were already at their places when the adults walked in. The room was large and high-ceilinged and could have been daunting with only five people at the table, but with bronze velvet curtains drawn across the windows, a huge fire burning in the hearth and a delicious aroma wafting from the soup tureen Mrs Ellis had just placed on the table, it was a welcoming scene. Still Helen couldn't repress a faint quiver of discomfort as she sank on to her seat. Last time she had come into this room she had been serving the dinner, carrying her aunt's delicious cooking through from the kitchen. It was a far from reassuring thought and she blocked the memory deliberately the moment it slipped into her mind, forcing herself to think of other things.

Tim had been placed between Matt and Katy at the table and he seemed to be completely relaxed and at his ease, talking to his father, explaining how he had managed to photograph the buzzards nesting on the ridge behind the cottage, the expression on his pale, intent face suddenly so painfully familiar to Helen that she drew in her breath and held it, hardly daring to move for a moment, sure that everyone else in the room must have seen the likeness between father and son that was so glaringly obvious to her. Steven's face had never worn that expression, so quietly serious, so absorbed and interested. He had been a cheerful, happy-go-lucky boy, taking life as it offered itself. Matt had always been the serious one in the Seymour family.

Helen dragged her gaze away from them at last, looking down at the table and crumbling the soft, home-made roll between her fingers in a vague pretence of eating. Had Matt or Mrs Seymour seen Tim with the same clear vision? she wondered. Were the events of the evening he had made love to her currently unfolding like video tape in Matt's brain? She had no real idea how the subconscious mind functioned but if anything could trigger off Matt's memory surely today's events must hold the key. So much had happened, and if their shared kiss hadn't been enough to unlock the secret recesses of his mind, surely Tim's face, wearing an expression he saw in the mirror every day, could quite well have done so.

But no, it seemed not. Dinner was over at last and almost immediately it was time for them to return to the cottage and nothing in Matt's demeanour led Helen to think that he saw her any differently now from when they had arrived. Mrs Ellis brought their coats and they stood in the large draughty hallway saying their goodbyes. Matt was behind Helen and even though she couldn't see him she was overwhelmingly conscious of his silent presence. Mrs Seymour moved forward, her hands on Helen's shoulders as she kissed her cheek.

'Good night, my dear,' she murmured, smiling gently and then she turned and said good night to Tim, one slender hand resting on his dark head for a moment. 'I've enjoyed your visit, Tim. Thank you for coming to see me.' She smiled down at him. 'You will come again, won't you?' she asked. Her voice was gentle but Helen's ultra-sensitive ears picked up the pleading note and her heart sank. She had been expecting this, armouring herself against it. How could they continue to visit Ellermere? It would be a tacit admission that Matt's suspicions about Tim were correct. And besides she had no wish to keep on meeting Matt Seymour. She had already seen far too much of him. It had to stop.

Mrs Seymour was looking at her now with faintly anxious brown eyes and she couldn't say any of the things she had planned. Instead she smiled weakly, prevaricating. 'It's difficult getting over here without a car, particularly during school term when Tim needs to go to bed early. Maybe in the school holidays ... perhaps we could come over then and spend the whole day with you and Katy.'

The moment she had spoken Helen felt like a heel. Madeline Seymour was trying to smile. 'That would be lovely, dear,' she said. But Helen knew she was upset and without turning her head she knew exactly what expression Matt's face would be wearing. She could feel the waves of disapproval emanating from his tall figure.

He moved then, ushering Helen and Tim towards the door, as though he couldn't bear to remain still or silent a moment longer. 'Leave the arrangements to me, Mother,' he said over his shoulder. 'Helen and I will sort something out on the way home.'

There was a hidden threat in his words and Helen

was not immune to it, although she told herself that whatever he said, whatever he did, nothing would persuade her to change her mind and she simply wouldn't allow him to bully her into doing anything she didn't want to do. She had half expected Tim to add his protests to Matt's once they were in the car, but the day's excitement seemed to have tired him out. He clambered into the back seat without a word and before they had been driving for five minutes he was asleep, his dark head nodding on the cream upholstery.

Matt was similarly non-committal. Helen stole a sideways glance at him but he was driving with concentrated attention, the hard edge of his perfect profile telling her nothing. She couldn't believe that he had given up so easily, but she felt too weary herself to worry about his probable actions. She let her head fall back against the seat and stared out of the window. The pale turquoise sky flickered in and out of the trees as Matt drove the car quickly over the icy, deserted roads. The stars were pale, barely visible, the moon an anaemic crescent, shedding little light. It had been a disturbing and exhausting day. Helen longed for the security of her own little cottage, the warmth and comfort of her fireside.

But when they finally reached the cottage, Matt walked up the path with them, a silent, brooding figure at Helen's side as she struggled to open the front door. The fire was still alight, she saw with relief from the doorway, the logs burning brightly, the small room seeming to reach out and welcome her. She turned abruptly.

'Thank you for bringing us home,' she murmured. She couldn't see Matt's face. He was just a tall, dark figure silhouetted against the pale, night sky until he spoke harshly to her.

'I think you know that we have things to discuss before I leave.'

Helen groaned inwardly. As she had thought, Matt was going to be difficult and she just hadn't the energy to cope with him this evening. 'Can't it wait?' she sighed. Tim was standing in the crook of her arm trying to keep his eyes open and she felt just as weary herself.

'Until the holidays, Helen?' Matt's voice was quiet but his tone cut like a whiplash through Helen's tired brain.

'I do have to work for a living, Matt, had you forgotten?' Tim seemed to have thrown off his tiredness in an instant, staring at them both with big eyes.

'You don't work in the evenings, Helen. Surely for my mother's sake you could manage a weekly visit.'

Helen sighed. She was simply too tired to think straight, but she did know it was impossible to continue this discussion with Tim, all ears at her side. 'You'd better come in,' she muttered ungraciously, moving aside reluctantly to let him pass. This was getting to be a habit and not one that she wanted to encourage. Taken in anything more than minute doses Matt Seymour was poison to her system. Surely she ought to know that by now.

Tim prepared for bed reluctantly, sensing from the strained atmosphere in the living room that he was going to miss something important. But he was ready at last, his blue eyes heavy with sleep as he smiled at Helen.

'Good night, Mum,' he mumbled.

She touched his soft hair gently, smiling down at him. 'Good night, Tim, sleep tight.'

Matt was standing beside her. He had taken off his jacket and was still wearing the formal business suit, his tall figure dominating the small room. But the power, the cool, cutting edge of his personality was sheathed when he spoke to Tim. There was only the charm and warmth visible then. 'Good night, Tim.' He flicked her son's cheek with a gentle finger and Helen looked away, biting her lip. Why did he have to come back into her life like this? They had been happy, just Tim and herself, but now she sensed that their lives would never be the same again.

'Good night, Uncle Matt.'

Helen had been gazing blank-eyed across the room but at that her head jerked around, her blue eyes flaring angrily. 'Tim, I don't think . . .' she began sharply. But Matt interrupted her, his tones silkily smooth.

'I gave permission for Tim to call me Uncle Matt. As we are to see quite a bit of one another in the future, it seemed reasonable enough.' His fingers were still resting on Tim's shoulders but his eyes challenged Helen openly across her son's head. He knew she was angry. He saw the way her eyes flashed fire at him but he also knew she couldn't do a thing about it, not with Tim watching every move she made.

'I see.' Helen forced herself to relax, smiling, although it had never been so hard. 'Go on up to bed now, love. I want to have a word with Mr Seymour. I promise I'll pop up and see you when he's gone.' She watched Tim's retreating figure, whirling on Matt furiously the moment she heard his bedroom door close behind him. 'Just don't go putting ideas into my son's head.' She shot the words at him like tiny daggers, every one intended to wound.

But he was impervious. 'And just what do you think you can do about it?' he asked, shrugging his shoulders, muscles rippling beneath the dark material of his suit.

Against her will Helen's eyes lingered on the

unconscious movement. She was far too aware of everything about him, she realised bitterly. His height and breadth, the darkly handsome features, the way his beautifully cut clothes fitted his lean-hipped figure. She wanted to look at him. She hated herself for that and her blue eyes flared even more angrily now as she glared at him furiously.

'We could go away, Tim and I. Leave the Lake District. We're not dependent on the almighty Seymours for a living. We're free agents, Matt. Had you forgotten?'

He didn't move but Helen fancied that his shadow seemed to grow in the dimly lit room. 'Run where you like, Helen, you seem to be good at that. You escaped your responsibilities once, but not this time. This time I'd be looking. This time I'd find you!'

Helen's laugh betrayed her incredulity. His words were so outrageous that for a moment she was lost for a reply. 'I escaped from my responsibilities!' she gasped. 'I think you must be crazy, Matt!' His hands were gripping her shoulders, but she didn't even notice she was so incensed.

'You can't deny that you were pregnant when you left Ellermere.'

Helen's lips were stubbornly tight. 'I do deny it, but even if I didn't, just let's suppose for a moment that your suspicions are correct. You're saying I ought to have stayed, involved your family in the ensuing scandal?'

'There would have been no scandal. Steven would have married you.'

'I didn't love Steven and he didn't love me!' Helen cried. 'Do you really think that would have been the answer?'

'Why not? Marriage to you wouldn't exactly have

been a penance,' Matt replied and Helen flushed vividly ·
as his dark eyes travelled over her.

'You would have married me under similar circumstances, I suppose?' Helen responded, rushing into
speech. 'A naïve, unsophisticated sixteen-year-old from
a totally different world. The cook's niece! It would
have looked great on the social pages of the glossy
magazines. Shares in Seymour stock would have
trebled, wouldn't they?' She was breathing quickly now
and she threw the words at him angrily.

'If I had made you pregnant I would have married
you, Helen,' he insisted.

'And blamed me ever afterwards,' she cried back at
him. 'But as Tim is not your brother's son, this whole
discussion is a waste of time.' Oh the irony of it, Helen
thought. This conversation was becoming impossible,
uncovering too many buried skeletons and it had to
stop right now. But clearly Matt had no intention of
allowing the subject to rest.

'Where would you go if you left the Lakes?' he
demanded with an intent look.

'You'd be the last person I'd tell!' Was he crazy,
Helen wondered? If she ran away it would be from him
she was running. Didn't he realise that?

'This Uncle Phil that you and Tim seem so wild
about, you'd go to him, I suppose?' Matt muttered
grimly and Helen flung back her head, blonde curls
swinging softly around her cheeks.

'Yes, I'd go to Philip,' Helen agreed.

Matt had been gripping her shoulders all this time
but only now did Helen notice, as they dug into her
flesh. 'Is he your lover? Is that why you won't come to
Ellermere? Is that why you're denying Tim's paternity?
In case he discovers the truth?'

'Philip knows all about Tim. He doesn't care who his

father is, he loves Tim anyway, just as he loves me!'
Helen cried.

'He loves you ... maybe, but not enough to marry
you, it seems.'

Helen's colour rose until her face flamed with it.
'Mind your own damned business!' she snapped.

'I'm making it my business. And whether your artist
friend approves or not, you are coming to visit my
mother again—soon. Resign yourself to the fact. She's
been ill. She isn't strong. I won't have her upset.'

They were very close, both breathing hard, their
angry glances clashing fiercely. 'I'm not coming to
Ellermere with you,' she cried. 'Haven't you realised yet
that I can't stand the sight of you? It would be
purgatory, seeing you every week, having to sit next to
you in the car. When you touch me I want to curl up
inside. I was revolted when you kissed me today. It
made me want to be sick!'

She faced him, still breathing fast, her face flushed,
her lips slightly parted, trembling with emotion and
before she could guess his intention, his dark head
swooped down to hers, his lips claiming her own,
moving over her mouth with a kind of brutal intensity
which made the trembling in her limbs so bad that she
could barely stand. She tried to keep her lips tightly
closed beneath that deliberate onslaught. She told
herself that he was bitterly angry with her and trying to
hurt her and she struggled fiercely, her body writhing
and twisting against his.

But it was a hopeless protest. He was too strong for
her, far too strong, and the bruising pressure of his
mouth was savage, relentless, forcing her lips apart, his
hands moving over her body with slow, insidious
caresses, moving up to her nape, tangling in her curls,
pressing her shaking body backward in the graceful,

helpless curve of a taut bowstring. She was totally at his mercy and unfortunately the longer he held her in his arms the more seductive his embrace was becoming.

Helen was on fire with long-buried passions, no longer even trying to pretend that she was immune to his kiss and when his mouth moved from her lips, sliding over the delicate curve of her cheekbone, covering her closed eyelids with tiny, possessive kisses, she moaned, a deep, husky murmur, her arms fastening around his neck with a small, convulsive jerk, all sensible thought completely banished from her head. So that when he raised his head at last, gazing down at her, she stared back helplessly, swaying on her feet, her eyes huge and bewildered in her flushed features.

'Well, if nothing else I seem to have proved a point,' he grated harshly, and she still continued to stare at him for a moment, the truth only slowly flickering to the surface of her dazed brain.

'I hate you, Matt Seymour,' she whispered on a trembling breath.

He shook his head, dark hair falling in a thick swathe over his forehead. 'So you keep telling me. But I think I've just proved that your word can't always be relied upon, don't you?' And before Helen could think of an answer to that he released her abruptly, moving across the room to collect his coat, turning as he reached the door, his dark eyes enigmatic as they rested on her trembling figure, still in the middle of the room.

'I won't insult your intelligence by apologising for that kiss. It happened! And God knows, you deserved it. You can't insult me for ever and expect to escape scot free.' His eyes surveyed her with faint mockery as he added. 'I shall be seeing you later, Helen. Shall we say Monday? I'll collect Tim from school as I did today.'

Helen felt as though she had been struck dumb, all the breath knocked out of her by his kiss and what had happened after. She stared at him like a zombie. She felt as though she had had an accident and was still suffering from shock. In fact it was some minutes after the porch door had finally closed behind Matt that she felt to have the strength to move and then she stumbled across to the sofa and collapsed weakly on to it, fierce wrenching sobs tearing through her body, tears running unheeded down her cheeks. Dimly she perceived, through the confusion in her brain, that something cataclysmic had happened to her today, something which couldn't easily be dismissed. She had reached a crossroads in her life. What did the future hold for her?

CHAPTER SEVEN

HELEN spent the next few days painting butterflies with a fierce concentration, intended to block out any other more disruptive thoughts and tire her out so thoroughly that she would fall asleep each night the moment her head touched the pillow. Her plan didn't work, of course: it failed abysmally to do so, and by Monday afternoon she was weary and heavy-eyed, suffering from a series of disturbed nights, Matt Seymour's tall figure appearing all too frequently in her restless dreams.

She was painting a huge, tropical species today and the iridescent blue of its wings seemed to blur and shimmer in front of Helen's eyes, so that she threw down her brush with a small, impatient gesture and pushing herself to her feet, walked over to the window, leaning her throbbing head against the cool, misted panes. The weather was doing nothing to help lighten her mood. It had rained steadily all night. She had heard it when she woke, just before dawn, dripping relentlessly from the overhanging eaves on to the corrugated roof of the small shed just below her window. And it was still raining, the sky a heavy, leaden pall of grey above the trees.

She sighed, rubbing her aching eyes as she walked over to the fire, piling more wood on to its smouldering embers. There was very little wind today and consequently the logs were burning sluggishly. Helen was cold, even though she was wearing two thick pullovers over her jeans. She felt a bit like a small animal roused too early from its winter sleep. Today she just wanted to hibernate, crouch in front of the fire with the door firmly shut against intruders and the thought of going to Ellermere in Matt Seymour's company filled her with dismay.

She liked Mrs Seymour and Katy very much, but remembering her last meeting with Matt she couldn't imagine how she was going to face him today with any degree of composure. The facts were both damning and inescapable. She had kissed him back! She had enjoyed it! She was a fool. Matt had used that kiss to punish her and she had let him. She ought to have pulled his hair or kicked his shins, done anything but give the response he had wanted. What price her protestations of immunity now? she reflected bitterly as she cleared away her paints, propping the still damp water-colour on the old-fashioned sideboard to dry. Clearly her only protection was to put as much space between herself and Matt as possible. But how could she do that? He knew where she lived and he was determined that she should continue to visit his home, if only for his mother's sake. And how could she fight him when he held all the cards? He said he didn't want to upset Tim but she had a feeling that if he didn't get his own way in this he would be ruthless, tell Tim everything.

Slowly Helen walked into the bathroom, stripping off her jeans and sweater to stand shivering on the cold tiles, waiting for the bath to fill. She was already worried about Tim and it was her son who occupied her thoughts as she climbed into the water and subsided thankfully beneath the warm, sweet-scented bubbles. He had talked of little else but 'Uncle' Matt and the Seymours for the past week. He was looking forward with unclouded pleasure to visiting Ellermere again, whistling cheerfully all the way to the bus stop this morning, completely unaffected by the driving rain or her own introspection.

His behaviour was disturbing. She never remembered him forming this close an attachment before, certainly not on such short acquaintance. Was there an unconscious bond between father and son which bound them together without either of them recognising the cause? Helen dismissed the idea instantly. The explanation was far more simple than that. Matt had set out to captivate her son, deliberately tried to win his affections and as she knew herself, when he chose to exert himself his charm could be lethal.

She climbed out of the bath, reaching for the towel, her slender body poised for a moment, graceful as a dancer's. And then she was drying herself briskly, the vigorous action briefly helping to dispel some of her more disturbing thoughts. She dressed quickly in a soft, blue, woollen frock which matched the colour of her eyes. It had long sleeves and a high buttoned neckline and she wore a pair of medium heeled, navy court shoes with it. She looked cool and sensible in the outfit, she decided, examining her outline in the wardrobe mirror. Was it a deliberate choice? she wondered. Was she subconsciously trying to discourage Matt from making any further advances? Simply because she knew that was her only defence, that if he once touched her, her response would be the same as last time. She would go weak at the knees and let him do exactly as he wanted with her.

That was some thought! And not one she wanted to encourage. She sat in front of the dressing table mirror, brushing her hair with vigorous strokes, almost welcoming the eye-watering pain when the bristles tangled in her curls. Her make-up was quickly completed. She wore very little, just a light coating of mascara, a slick of pale grey shadow on her eyelids, a fresh coral lipstick, and then she was ready. It was exactly three-forty-five as she walked down the stairs, carrying her raincoat over one arm and she could hear the deep throbbing note of a car engine as it climbed the hill towards the cottage.

They were here already! She would have liked to be cool and icily composed, or at least present a façade of composure, but instead she had a nasty, sick feeling in the pit of her stomach and her hands were so clammy that the strap of her handbag felt sticky in her palm. But when Tim opened the door she was already throwing her raincoat over her shoulders and she looked towards it, forcing a bright smile to her stiffened lips. But one glance at his face told her that something was wrong. All the excitement, the cheerful insouciance of the morning had completely disappeared. There was an unfamiliar droop to his lower lip and he couldn't quite disguise the wobble in his voice as he said, 'The car's here, Mum. It's a Rolls Royce. But Uncle Matt couldn't make it. He's busy. He sent Mr Waddington instead.'

Helen's first reaction was one of intense relief, but still she smiled sympathetically at her son as they walked out to the car. 'Maybe we'll see him later, love,' she consoled him. 'Maybe he'll be at Ellermere when we arrive.'

But he wasn't, not that week, or the next, or the one after and Helen's pleasure and relief at his absence began to dissipate rapidly. Mrs Seymour told her one day that his factories had been sent a mammoth order from the States for some very specialised piece of mining equipment and everyone was working long hours. Helen wasn't convinced. When she arrived home that night she sat for a long time in front of the dying fire busy with her own thoughts. She simply couldn't believe Mrs Seymour's explanation. It was too simple— too pat. She felt sure that Matt was playing a very subtle game of cat and mouse with her. He wasn't in full possession of the facts, of course. He didn't know why she was so wary of him. But he was sensitive enough to recognise that she was frightened. Was he playing on that fear? Deliberately drawing out the suspenses. Making her wonder and worry just when he was going to pounce, as an additional punishment for the angry words she had hurled at him? Or worse still, had he decided to wash his hands of the whole troublesome subject? Had he decided that it was Steven's problem, after all and put all the facts in front of his brother, leaving him to deal with it? If so her troubles would just be beginning. Steven would deny that they had ever been lovers, and just what would Matt make of that?

It wasn't a comfortable subject to take to bed with her and she slept very badly, tossing and turning half the night, staggering downstairs after the alarm rang, still half asleep.

It didn't help her mood when Tim said to her, over the breakfast table, 'Uncle Matt never spends any time with us now and it's no fun without him. Why don't we see him anymore?' He was wading through a huge bowl of cornflakes and he lifted his head, his laden spoon poised half-way to his mouth, waiting for Helen to answer.

She shook her head, running a distracted hand through her tangled curls. 'We're only visitors at Ellermere, Tim. Matt's a busy man. We have no real claim on his time.'

Tim clearly wasn't convinced by her reasoning and his face was almost mutinous as he gazed up at her. 'He likes being with us, I know he does. Can't we invite him for tea some time, just the three of us, like before?'

Helen groaned silently, gazing at the embroidered tablecloth as though it might suddenly and miraculously provide her with inspiration. If only Tim knew what he was asking. But then again, maybe it was a good thing he didn't. There were so many undercurrents in her relationship with Matt Seymour, true explanations were impossible and she was growing increasingly tired of having to give evasive answers. She raised her head, her eyes gentle as they rested on her son's unhappy face. 'What about Katy and Mrs Seymour? Don't you think they would be hurt if we issued an invitation which didn't include them? And we simply don't have room to entertain them all comfortably.'

Tim conceded the point with reluctance but he wasn't happy and he left for school with a very gloomy face. 'We can't go on like this,' Helen told the empty room after she had taken him to the bus stop. 'Something will have to be done.' Unfortunately she still had no clear idea just what that something would be.

Towards the end of March the weather began to improve noticeably. Crocuses blossomed in Helen's tiny front garden at Fell Cottage and now that her butterfly illustrations were completed, she spent more time out of doors, painting the landscapes which were her special joy. The craft shop owner in Ambleside, who sold some of her work, was delighted with the pictures she took to him, and insisted on buying her lunch at one of the nicer restaurants in town. He was a bearded, plump man in shabby trousers and a comfortable sweater and he loved his little shop, tucked away in one of the back streets. He would never make a fortune but he was happy and it showed on his smiling face as he looked at Helen over the white tablecloth.

'If you keep your prices reasonably steady I can sell whatever you produce,' he promised cheerfully.

Helen ought to have been overjoyed. The margin of profit she made was adequate. Painting landscapes in water-colour was the work she enjoyed best. But her mood was strangely subdued. She summoned up a bright smile for Edward Leach's benefit but she couldn't feel any real pleasure in her achievements. Even painting had temporarily lost its charm. She was in a rut, she decided as she sat in the bus on the way home from Ambleside. She needed a change. And yet, hadn't her life always been quiet and uneventful? Her social contacts were practically non-existent. Apart from Philip Ackroyd, her only real friends were Mr and Mrs Williams, her neighbours. The women of her own age in the village were all married, with husbands living at home. As a single parent she had always felt different, held herself slightly aloof but her solitary state had never troubled her, until now.

She knew what was wrong with her, of course. She was letting Matt Seymour get under her skin. His continued absence was proving far more disturbing than his physical presence would have been. How he would laugh if he knew. She stared out of the window, for once immune to the beauty of the passing scene. Almost every garden along the bus route was bright with spring bulbs, jasmine was in flower, mingling with the bright scarlet berries of cotoneaster, but she didn't notice any of this. Just what was Matt Seymour's purpose in staying away from them? She couldn't believe he had taken her words to heart and decided to leave them alone for that reason. No, his motives must be entirely different. But how could she protect herself against them when she had no idea what they were?

She was still mulling over the same problem when the

bus dropped her at the edge of Hawksmoor village. It had been ten minutes behind schedule and she hurried towards the school, guessing that Tim would already be waiting for her. She saw his small figure in the bright red anorak the moment she turned the corner and she waved cheerfully, running towards him.

'I'm sorry I'm late,' she gasped. 'Have you been waiting long?'

'About five minutes,' Tim admitted. Helen thought there was something oddly subdued about his reply but she didn't have time to stop and question him just then. The coach which ran past their cottage only did so at infrequent intervals and she knew there was one due at any time.

'Come on, Tim,' she said. 'Let's try and catch the bus. I feel too weary to walk up Cop Hill today.'

They sped along the main street of the village, arriving at the bus stop just as the driver was starting the engine. 'Practising for the Garton Fell Race, are you love?' he asked, grinning down at Helen's tangled curls and flushed cheeks.

She laughed back, her blue eyes dancing, too breathless to answer him. She was out of condition, she decided, as she collapsed on to the maroon leather seat. But Tim was looking more cheerful now. He had some colour in his cheeks and he seemed to have forgotten whatever had been troubling him.

'Mr Henshaw's going to take part in the fell race,' he remarked as the bus began to roar along the quiet village street. 'He's going to send a letter to everyone in the school, asking us to sponsor him, so we can buy a computer.'

Helen smiled. Mr Henshaw was the headmaster of the village school. She had always found him rather reserved, difficult to talk to, but the children all adored him, and Tim was no exception. 'If you bring a letter home, of course I'll sponsor him,' she promised. 'And maybe you could ask Mr and Mrs Williams as well.'

Tim looked pleased and he sat in silence for the rest of the short journey, watching out of the window. The bus stop was half way up the hill. 'Don't forget, keep practising your sprint finish,' the driver called, smiling down at them, his eyes lingering appreciatively on Helen's slim, jean clad figure at the side of the road. Helen smiled back and Tim waved as the bus roared up the hill in a cloud of exhaust smoke. Helen was still smiling to herself as she and Tim trudged up the path towards the cottage. The driver's obvious admiration had been good for her morale. She knew she would have run a mile if he'd tried a more determined approach but it was reassuring to know that she could still attract the opposite sex on occasion. Providing that was as far as it went.

The ground under the trees was damp, boggy in places, the smell of wet vegetation almost overpowering. But everywhere that Helen looked there were definite signs that spring was on the way. The buds on the oak trees were still tightly furled, but they were fat, full of new life, just waiting to split open and reveal the bright green leaves packed so tightly inside. She could see bluebell leaves pushing determinedly towards the light, and already the wood anemones were in flower, tiny white stars against the background of last year's fallen leaves.

Despite her earlier depression Helen felt her spirits beginning to rise. She was even humming to herself, a catchy little tune she'd heard on the radio that morning and Tim's muttered words didn't sink in at first. But something in his voice made her turn her head and look at him sharply and she noticed for the first time that he had the beginnings of a bruise on his forehead, beneath the dark hair, and his red anorak was stained with mud at the back, as though he had been fighting.

'What did you say, love?' she asked.

He looked up at her, a certain defiance in his stance as he muttered, 'What does bastard mean, Mum?'

Helen's breath caught in her throat, the colour draining from her cheeks, all pleasure in the mild, spring afternoon completely dissipated. She realised that her feet had stopped moving automatically but now she forced herself to stride forward again. 'Why do you ask, Tim?' she murmured, trying to keep her voice level. But she knew why, of course, before he answered her.

He shrugged, his head drooping as he kicked disconsolately at the wet leaves underfoot. 'Billy Ashwood and horrible Darren Selden called me that today. We had a fight,' he confessed in a mumble, because he knew Helen disapproved of the casual bullying some boys seemed to indulge in. 'But they started it,' he insisted, raising his head now, his blue eyes sparkling defiantly. 'I punched Darren Selden on the nose and made it bleed, and I'm glad! They've been teasing me for days. It's just because Uncle Matt sends Waddington to collect me in the Rolls. They're jealous!'

They both stopped walking and Helen stared down at her son's bent head, her eyes huge and dark, filled with pain. It was her fault. Why hadn't she realised what would happen? She ought to have known that the people in Hawksmoor village weren't blind. The Seymour family were well known in the area. Matt would be a familiar figure to most of them. The fact that he had known Mr and Mrs Willims ought to have warned her of that. Tim was very like his father, and once their regular visits to Ellermere began, people had clearly started to watch her slim, dark haired son with fresh eyes and she had been too self-absorbed to see it coming, too concerned with her own problems, her own reactions, to consider other people's response. But it was far too late for self-recrimination now, she realised. The damage was done. The question now was how to explain it to Tim without making the situation worse. He was clearly hurt and bewildered. He didn't know the meaning of the word they'd so cruelly thrown at him but he knew it was an insult and he had also realised that somehow it was connected with Matt.

She touched his hair gently. It was so like his father's, she thought emotionally, it even felt like Matt's when she touched it, soft and thick. She had tangled her fingers in his hair when he had kissed her and the memory made her eyes darken with anguish. She had been a fool to stay here once Matt had found them. But she had been torn both ways, knowing she ought to run away but not wanting to go. It was almost a relief now to have no choice. For Tim's sake they would have to leave. Go back to Manchester. Seek the anonymity of the big city. She had been silent so long that Tim raised his head, watching her and she sighed, collecting her straying thoughts with an effort.

'It's a difficult situation, Tim,' she told him gently. 'I'm sure you're right about Billy and his friend. They are jealous. But it's not just the Rolls, that's only a symptom.' She smiled encouragingly, looking at his smooth, young face, wondering if he understood even half of what she was trying to say to him. 'I think they probably resent our friendship with the Seymours,' she continued quietly. 'They are an old and distinguished family. They have been landowners, very important people in this area, for generations. We are obviously not from their world. Some people might think we were

getting above ourselves, being on terms of friendship
with them.'

Even if Tim didn't understand completely, Helen's
explanation seemed to help. He was quiet for a moment
but then he raised his head. 'I'm sorry I burst Darren's
nose, Mum.'

Helen saw his anxious little face and longed to hug
him. Darren Selden's bloody nose was the least of her
worries at the moment. 'Would you like me to come
into school in the morning and speak to the teacher?'
she asked.

But Tim shook his head, fiercely vetoing the
suggestion. And after that he seemed to put the subject
out of his mind completely, making no attempt to
question Helen further. But sooner or later Helen knew
that it would come to light again. One of the children in
the village would hear his parents talking and oblige
Tim with a much fuller and far more wounding
explanation than she had just given him. Until now he
had accepted the brief details Helen had invented about
her divorced husband, without undue curiosity. But if
he began to question her in earnest she was uncertain
that she could keep up the pretence. Tim would be
confused and hurt at the very least and Helen knew
they both had to disappear before that could happen.

Next morning she took Tim all the way to school
determined to set events in motion for their departure.
The thought of leaving Fell Cottage was a painful one.
But the world had intruded and even the solid walls of
their sturdy little house couldn't keep it out any longer.
A clean break would be best, she told herself firmly. It
would be sad for them both. But staying would be
worse. And to make doubly sure that this time she
didn't weaken, she had written to her landlord the
previous evening, telling him they would be leaving his

cottage and she popped the letter into the post box immediately after leaving Tim outside school.

She had some shopping to do at the small village store and she went there next. She was the only customer this early in the morning, which was something of a relief. Mrs Langdon was a kindly soul but she loved to gossip. She was never malicious but she had been born in a cottage very near to Madeline Seymour and the whole family seemed to fascinate her. Once she realised Helen knew them, that was it, she never wanted to talk about anyone else and they were the last subject Helen wanted to discuss in front of an audience.

'I remember Madeline Seymour when she was just a lass,' she had told Helen only last week. 'She had all the young gentlemen from miles around in love with her. Eh, it was romantic.' And Mrs Langdon's face took on a wistful, far-away expression as she added, 'Edward Seymour fell in love the moment he clapped eyes on her, so they do say. But her parents weren't that keen, would you believe? They were aiming high, a duke or an earl was what they had in mind for Madeline. She had a grand London season, all the toffs chasing her, but she still came home and married Mr Edward.' Mrs Langdon nodded and smiled when she told Helen this. It was her idea of a happy ending. And Mr Edward had been a better catch in her view than any London toff. 'He was a real gentleman,' she told Helen. 'And Mr Matt and Mr Steven, they're as like him as two peas in a pod.'

She came puffing out of the room at the back of the shop now, as the door bell clanged, and Helen smiled at her. 'Good morning, Mrs Langdon,' she said. 'How are you feeling today?'

She looked blooming with health, her plump cheeks

ruddy, but Helen knew she was very overweight and suffered from high blood pressure. She had been told to go on a diet by her doctor. 'But I couldn't do with starving myself at my age.' So she had told Helen. 'I'm too old to change,' she laughed, wheezing a little. 'I'll keep on eating and die happy.' And she was beaming cheerfully now. 'Can't complain. Just my usual troubles. But I'll surprise that doctor of mine yet. Now, what can I get for you, Mrs Delaney?'

Helen gave her the list she'd prepared and Mrs Langdon bustled off to collect the items from the shelves. Shopping had always been a problem in Hawksmoor. There were no supermarkets, so Helen was forced to pay full price for everything. And bus fares were so expensive that she would have been out of pocket had she travelled into one of the bigger towns every week to buy her groceries. But now she looked round the small shop with saddened eyes. The shelves were packed tight. Mrs Langdon sold everything you could think of. She was going to miss the friendly atmosphere, she realised. She would miss so many things . . .

Mrs Langdon came back at that moment, distracting Helen's thoughts. 'That's your sugar and tea,' she puffed, placing the packets on the steadily growing pile in front of Helen. 'I'll just fetch your bread from the back. They've already delivered but I haven't had time to unpack.' She was back almost immediately with a crusty loaf and a packet of brown rolls. They were Tim's favourite. He loved to eat them with mushroom soup. Looking at the pile of groceries on the counter Helen realised that unconsciously she had been buying all the items he liked best. It was going to upset him when she told him they were leaving Hawksmoor. She was buying his favourite foods as a kind of sop to her own conscience. Not that she wanted to leave herself. It wasn't going to be easy for either of them. Hawksmoor was home. And at this moment she felt as though she would never be happy anywhere else.

'Will that be all?' Mrs Langdon was asking now. 'I've got some lovely ham on the bone, just home in from the wholesaler's,' she added hopefully.

Helen shook her head. 'No, not today, thanks. I think I've bought everything I need.' She opened her purse and took out two five pound notes, pushing them across the counter. She couldn't afford ham on the bone, not now, not with all the expenses of removal to meet. They would have to stay in digs in Manchester until they could find a small flat. And she had already decided that she would have to hire a small van to help with the removal. There was no way they could carry all their luggage with them on the bus.

The till drawer flew open. 'Are you going to Ellermere today?' Mrs Langdon asked, unaware that she was treading sensitive ground. 'The woods round the house will be beautiful just now I expect, coming into leaf. I remember we went to a garden party there once, me and my Alf. The roses were a picture. Aye, and Mrs Seymour saw me admiring them and gave me a bunch. She wouldn't take no for an answer. Fairly forced them on to me,' Mrs Langdon said, beaming across the counter at Helen as she handed her the change. 'It came to seven pounds thirty-eight, dear, so there's two pounds and sixty-two change. See you soon,' she called as Helen opened the door and hurried out. She hadn't been able to control her heightened colour when Mrs Langdon had mentioned the Seymours and if she was going to be overcome with embarrassment every time someone mentioned their name she had better leave Hawksmoor even sooner than she had planned. Not everyone was as self-absorbed as Mrs Langdon. That sort of stupid behaviour would simply confirm their worst suspicions.

She hurried along the village street knowing what her next task must be, and dreading it. She had to let Madeline Seymour know of her decision and if she didn't ring today she doubted whether she would have sufficient courage ever again. She went into the 'phone booth outside the small post office and slowly lifted the receiver, clutching it tightly in her left hand as she dialled the number. Her first instinct had been simply to disappear, lose herself and Tim in the sprawling suburbs of the big city. But then she thought of the pain that would inflict on Mrs Seymour and Katy and she just couldn't do it. And surely even Matt would see that they couldn't continue living at Hawksmoor under the circumstances.

The ringing tones went on and on but at last someone picked up the receiver. 'Matt Seymour here.' And the deep, masculine voice seemed to send a shiver down Helen's spine. It was weeks since she had seen Matt and she stared at the receiver for a moment in total silence, but Matt was becoming impatient now. 'Who is that please?' he asked brusquely, and Helen gulped, taking a deep, steadying breath, knowing that if she hadn't been desperate to speak to Madeline Seymour she would simply have slammed the 'phone down and fled.

'It's Helen, Helen Delaney,' she murmured tremulously. It was his turn to be silent now and even though Helen was alone in the telephone box she could feel her colour rising. She could almost hear his brain ticking over, almost hear his silent thoughts.

'How can I help you, Helen?' he asked at last, his

tone cool and guarded and Helen had to force herself to answer him, her throat so tight it hurt to speak.

'Could I have a word with your mother, please?' she croaked.

'I'm sorry, my mother's in bed with a heavy cold. Is there anything I can do to help?' Maybe it was Helen's imagination but his cool voice seemed the opposite of encouraging and unbidden, a sigh came to Helen's lips.

'No, no I don't think so, thanks,' she murmured. There was no way she was going to launch into a lengthy explanation for this man's benefit. 'Would you just tell her that Tim and I can't come to Ellermere on Monday. I—I'll ring later, when she's feeling better, and explain.'

'Are either of you ill?' he demanded sharply.

'We're okay,' Helen muttered, but she couldn't repress another faint sigh. She was far from okay. In fact she felt totally depressed, as though the odds were all stacked against her. Not that she was going to say that to Matt. 'Tell your mother not to worry, Tim's perfectly well, and as I said, I'll ring later and explain.'

But Matt was far from satisfied with her answer. 'Explain to me now, Helen,' he barked.

Helen shook her head, although she knew he couldn't see her. 'No . . . no, I can't, I'm sorry . . . the bus,' she stammered disjointedly. 'I shall have to run. I'll ring later.' She slammed the receiver down and hurried out of the booth, leaning against the door for a moment to allow her breathing to return to normal.

It had been upsetting talking to Matt, for more reasons than one. She hadn't realised until now just how much she had missed him over the past few weeks. When she had heard his voice on the telephone she had felt a tremendous urge to burst into tears and pour out all her troubles and if he had been a little friendlier she suspected she would have done just that. She began to walk, striding up the hill out of the village, the heavy shopping bags which she always seemed to be burdened with, dragging her arms out of the sockets. There had been no bus due, of course. That was just an excuse to escape from Matt before she broke down and cried in his ear. She didn't understand why she felt so wretched suddenly. Life had thrown plenty of difficulties in her way but she had always managed to cope with them in the past. All her problems seemed to have come to a head at once, just at a time when she felt least able to manage. The truth was, she didn't want to move. She loved the Lakes. She loved the cottage. She had wonderful neighbours and both she and Tim had become attached to Mrs Seymour and Katy. It would be a painful wrench to return to Manchester.

She was scarlet cheeked and panting by the time she had walked half way up the hill and she kept having to stop and put down her carrier bags, give her aching fingers and arms a rest. The sky was a pale, misty grey this morning but she was still too hot, stifling in her padded anorak. The road climbed up the hill between a belt of trees at this point and there was not the faintest breath of wind to stir their branches. Helen stopped again, unfastening her jacket, pausing to look back the way she had come. The road curved but the houses in Hawksmoor were still visible through the bare branches of the trees, woodsmoke curling lazily from their chimneys.

She bent her head, picking up her bags, tears suddenly smarting behind her eyelids. She was a fool, becoming morbid. Living at Hawksmoor hadn't been so damned perfect. Tim's recent experience had proved that. Some of the villagers were parochial and narrow minded, and as for being upset at leaving the Seymours, that showed how stupidly she was behaving, because surely Matt Seymour and his family were the cause of all her problems in the first instance. She trudged up the road trying to think her sensible thoughts but before too long she was simply too tired to think at all. The long winter hibernation had taken its toll, and her body was protesting at the unaccustomed exercise but she forced her feet to keep moving. Birds sang in the woods. The sun came out, the grey clouds parting to reveal a sky of delicate, eggshell blue but Helen's head was down, her tangled hair lying damply over her forehead and she was far too weary to notice.

She wasn't even aware of the powerful car roaring up the hill behind her, and when it slowed to a halt just in front, its engine throbbing on a deep, even note she didn't look up at first. Hawksmoor was on the tourist track. People were always stopping to gaze at the view. It was Matt's voice saying her name which halted her in her tracks. He had climbed half out of the Range Rover, twisting to look at her, one lean hand gripping the roof, staring at her with hooded, angry eyes. And Helen stared back, laden carrier bags clutched in both hands, her face flooding with painful colour. Oh no! she thought wildly. This is all I need! Stupidly she could already feel her eyes filling with tears, but she bit her lip fiercely, willing them away.

His face was still unsmiling. He didn't speak again. He just walked towards her, the car door swinging behind him as he took the bags from her unresisting fingers, putting them carefully into the back seat before opening the passenger door and propelling her towards it. She went with him helplessly, feeling a bit like a robot under remote control. He still hadn't said a word but she could tell he was furiously angry and she began to tremble, all her concentration bent on trying to hide it from him. He had slid in beside her now. She knew he was watching her but she didn't turn around, his figure a dark, formidable shape, glimpsed from the corner of her eye.

'Sometimes the urge to put you over my knee and spank you becomes almost uncontrollable,' he muttered at last in a harsh, over-controlled voice. 'Are you crazy, or what?' He was breathing hard, his control slipping now, anger flaring in his tones. 'Why the hell can't you behave like any other normal, sensible human being? Are you a masochist, is that it? Does it give you a kick to inflict as much pain as possible on yourself and everyone around you?'

Helen closed her eyes tightly, trembling inside, the irony, the injustice of Matt's words striking her like a blow. 'Don't,' she whispered. 'Please don't.' And then to her shock and horror she burst into tears, wild, uncontrollable tears which poured down her cheeks, trickling over the fingers she pressed to her eyes, dripping unchecked on to the dark blue material of her anorak. This couldn't be her, she thought wildly. She never cried! It was a weakness that she simply couldn't afford. But she was crying now, her shoulders shaking, her whole body racked with painful, wrenching sobs. Matt simply sat and stared at her in stunned disbelief for a moment and then he reached out, strong hands on her shoulders, pulling her into his arms.

'Christ . . . Helen! What's wrong! What's happened? I knew when I answered the 'phone that something had upset you. What can I do? Tell me!'

His suit jacket had fallen open and Helen's face was pressed tight against the soft material of his shirt, but she didn't try to pull away. It was warm and secure in his arms. His heart was thudding with stong, regular beats against her cheek and he smelled delicious too, expensive aftershave mingling with the clean, warm smell of his body. She felt like a child again. She wanted to cling to him tightly, wind her arms around his neck and behave in a totally idiotic fashion. He stroked her hair, his fingers moving gently among her tangled curls and gradually, as Helen's tears subsided, harsh reality began to intrude. She was locked tightly in Matt Seymour's embrace on the main road out of Hawksmoor village, traffic was increasing by the minute and as she became calmer her response needed to lying in his arms was far from being that of a child. She wanted him to kiss her again. A deep, physical hunger was growing inside her. She wanted his lean hands to caress her body. She wanted him to make love to her and the feeling was almost uncontrollable.

She practically tore herself out of his arms, trembling at the shocked recognition of her own weakness, fearing she had given away some hint of the tormenting, tumultuous emotions locked so painfully in her own head. He was still a wildly attractive man and she couldn't help being aware of that fact, she told herself in silent apology. But it didn't help. She bent her head, searching blindly for a tissue, her fingers shaking as she strove to disguise that fact from Matt's curious gaze.

'What's wrong, Helen?' he asked again.

'I'd rather not discuss it,' she whispered, turning her head, gazing blindly in front of her, fighting for composure. Matt had wound his window down and the warm, pungent smell of early spring drifted into the car, bringing with it the liquid song of a blackbird. Unbidden tears were springing to Helen's eyes once again.

Matt was still watching her. 'You'd better tell me. If you think I'm about to drive away and leave you in this state, you're mistaken. I know that your opinion of me isn't particularly high. You've made that perfectly clear in the past. But for my mother's sake if nothing else, I intend to get to the bottom of this.'

'There's nothing you can do,' Helen said, feeling a ridiculous desire to burst into tears once again. Why was he being so kind to her? She had been so sure he intended to punish her for the horrible things she had said to him. She had unconsciously been dreading the form his punishment would take. But now she realised that his kindness was worse. It weakened her when she needed to be strong. At this moment it would have been wonderful to simply lay her head back on Matt's powerful shoulders and pour out all her troubles, let him make all the decisions. But it just wouldn't do. Tomorrow, when she felt more her old self again, she would resent his interference. She was too independent. She had always had to be. 'Stand on your own two feet. Don't depend on anyone.' Aunt Lily had drilled that into her as a child. She had never forgotten.

Matt was staring at her with frustrated eyes. 'I'm not letting you out of this car until you explain exactly what's been going on.'

Something in his tone made Helen turn her head and look at him then. He meant exactly what he said, she realised, seeing his set expression. 'Please Matt,' she murmured huskily. 'There's nothing you can do, and it's not something I want to discuss.'

His eyes locked on to hers. 'I mean to know. You may as well tell me immediately, because believe me we shall both stay here until you do.'

'You can't keep me here against my will,' Helen protested weakly.

'Just try me,' he offered, his dark brows raised above eyes which issued a direct challenge. 'Tell me what's troubling you. You will in the end!'

Helen stared out of the window blindly, already

secretly accepting that she would do as he asked, but
still unwilling to admit the truth. Just what would his
reaction be if she did tell him? she wondered. He would
be angry for Tim's sake, of course, but would he also be
secretly pleased that his own theory as to Tim's
paternity had apparently been confirmed. She bit her
lip, knowing that she had to speak sometime.

'It's Tim,' she muttered at last, realising there was no
point in prevaricating any longer and once she'd started
it was easy to carry on and she told him the whole,
unpleasant story in quiet, level tones which said nothing
of the turmoil in her own head. 'That's why we won't
be coming to Ellermere on Monday. I'm intending to
move next week. Tim will be ... upset.' Her voice
faltered on the words, but she carried on after a
moment. 'A quick, clean break will be best. He can start
at his new school in Manchester after the Easter
holidays.'

Matt had lit a cheroot whilst she was speaking but
now he stabbed it out in the ashtray with one vicious,
angry movement. 'My God,' he breathed, 'the little
devils. If I could get my hands on them.' He frowned
now, his eyes intent. 'What about Tim? Is he okay?'

Helen shrugged, her eyes on the faint thread of
smoke still spiralling from the half smoked cheroot in
the ashtray. 'He was upset at first, naturally, but he
seemed to be much better this morning. And as for Billy
and Darren, I don't suppose they realised exactly what
they were saying. They were simply repeating something
they'd heard. Everyone is talking, I'm afraid. Obviously
we can't stay here. We have to leave,' she added, faint
desperation in her tones.

'I agree, you must.' Matt had himself under control
again and he moved suddenly, flicking the ignition,
gunning the powerful engine into life. 'But you are not

going to Manchester.' He paused, looking in his mirror before easing the car back on to the road. 'Ellermere's half empty these days. You can come and live there. My mother and Katy will both welcome the company.'

CHAPTER EIGHT

HELEN was aghast, unable to believe in that first moment that she had really heard the words he uttered. The car was roaring up the hill but she hardly noticed. She stared at him, her blue eyes wide and shocked. 'You can't be serious,' she gasped.

He shot her a brief, sideways glance, seeing the shock, the total incredulity written on her face, and ignoring it. 'Why shouldn't I be serious?' he asked. 'It seems an eminently sensible suggestion to me.'

Helen moved her head slowly backwards and forwards. Was he crazy? It was the most ridiculous suggestion she had ever heard. 'Haven't you listened to a single word I've said?' She slumped back in her seat, her eyes closed, as though the matter of fact expression on his hard features was one she simply didn't want to register. 'If we came to live at Ellermere, what would happen then? Just what do you think people would say?'

'I don't know, and believe me I don't really care,' Matt responded coolly, taking a sharp left turn, the speed of the car slowing as the wheels encountered the roughly surfaced road leading to Helen's cottage.

'You may not care, but then it's not you who's going to have to face the gossip, is it?' Helen countered instantly, glaring at him.

'There won't be any difficulties,' he told her patiently. 'Tim will go to the same school as Katy. My mother had a large family and as far as anyone knows you can have been married to her nephew or some other distant

relation. That would explain Tim's physical appearance
to everyone's satisfaction.' His voice took on a harder
note. 'Unless of course you want to stick to your old
story. Tell everyone that the likeness is a mere
coincidence. That Tim has, somehow, through some
strange genetic accident, inherited Seymour features
without having a member of the family in his
ancestry.'

'I don't want to discuss it,' Helen sighed. 'The whole
thing is ridiculous.' The car had slowed to a halt in
front of the cottage and she would have stumbled out
but he put his hand on her arm, restraining her.

'Forget that you hate me, Helen. Forget everything
except what's best for your son. You can't stay in
Hawksmoor, I would agree. Both your lives would be
impossible. But think a minute. Exactly what sort of
existence would you be able to give him in Manchester?
Living in some poky little flat. Taking him to school in
an inner city suburb where the teacher is too busy trying
to quell the livelier spirits to have time to teach more
than the basic necessities. He's a bright boy, Helen.
Anyone can see that. You'd be denying him the future
he deserves, and you know it.' He had dropped his arm
but he was staring into her eyes, not allowing her to
look away.

With a tremendous effort Helen dropped her eyes.
'We'll go to Philip,' she said now on a trembling breath.
'He's away, painting in Spain at the moment but the
moment he comes back we'll go to him. He loves Tim. I
know he'll want us to stay with him.' But in her heart
she knew that without realising the full story Matt was
in the right. Because she would never be able to bring
herself to tell Matt the complete truth she wasn't being
fair to Tim. She was denying him so many things . . .
But what else could she do? She certainly couldn't

accept his offer of a home for them both at Ellermere. The surge of hope she'd felt when Matt had first invited her had been a warning. It had shaken her. To even consider his offer would be madness. How could she live in the same house after all that had happened between them? She was older, and she hoped a little wiser than when she had left Ellermere ten years ago, but still, it would be crazy to tempt fate a second time.

Her head was still bent but still she knew he was watching her, his tones perceptibly harder since she had mentioned Philip's name. 'So, until your friend comes home from Spain you aim to drag Tim off to live in a seedy bedsit?'

Helen raised her shoulders helplessly, her voice husky as she said: 'Matt, I don't know ... you're not being fair ... there are so many things to consider.' Too many things and she felt as though, in the space of a few seconds, she had considered them all. She was suddenly intensely weary. Far too weary to protest any longer. Besides, what else could she say to him? I'm sorry, we can't come to Ellermere because I still seem to be far too susceptible to tall, dark men like you. The idea was ridiculous and yet wasn't the alternative Matt was offering completely unthinkable?

'Come to Ellermere, Helen,' Matt whispered persuasively as though he sensed her weakness. 'If you want to move to Manchester when your friend returns to the country, I give you my word I shan't try to stop you.'

It was very quiet in the car with the engine turned off. Matt continued to watch her, his dark eyes fixed on her delicate profile. Helen stared out of the window at the familiar, dark, slate walls of her little cottage, the faint whisper of blue-grey smoke still curling lazily out of the chimney. Philip had bought her a large pottery urn last summer and she had filled it with bulbs. They were in flower now, tiny, jewel-bright crocuses, slender irises, the last of the snowdrops, spreading their petals wide, making the best of the early spring sunshine.

'I wouldn't be very much in evidence. If that's what's making you hesitate.' Matt's husky voice came from behind her averted head now and Helen gave a tiny shiver of mingled fear and excitement as she felt the warmth of his breath on her slender neck.

'I'm a busy man. I'm often away for days at a time. My mother and Katy are on their own then. I would feel happier if they had company, if I knew you were with them.' For a few moments longer Matt's voice wore away at the frail roots of Helen's determination with the persistence of water dripping off a stone. And then he fell silent, waiting, and when Helen still didn't answer he gave a short, muttered exclamation. 'For God's sake! I meant what I said. I will leave you completely alone if that's what you want. You can't deny that I've kept my distance these past weeks. It would be no different if you were living in the house. I know you don't like me, can't stand the sight of me, in fact. Isn't that what you said?' he asked, a thread of bitterness underlying his harsh tones and against all reason stirring Helen's compassion.

She had frequently told herself that the cruel words she had flung at him were entirely necessary, but now, looking at his taut expression, she felt ashamed. 'I'm sorry. I said an awful lot of things to you ... most of which I didn't mean,' she admitted huskily. 'But you made me very angry.'

'I certainly got that impression.' Matt's tone was wry but Helen could almost feel the taut lines of his body relaxing beside her.

'You seemed to think you could walk right back into my life and take charge of everything.'

'Crazy isn't it?' Matt agreed, laughing softly, sounding as though he couldn't quite believe it himself. 'But that's the effect you had on me, Helen. Even before I saw Tim. I took one look at those big, anxious, blue eyes and wanted to take you under my wing.'

There was something in Matt's dark, husky tones which Helen had to force herself to ignore. 'I don't want protecting, Matt, haven't you realised that yet? I've always had to manage on my own and that's the way I like it.' Helen dared not meet Matt's eyes. She was lying in her teeth and she was afraid he would be able to read the truth on her face. She had always had to depend on herself, that was true enough, but that didn't mean she liked it. The thought of being cosseted and protected by Matt Seymour had a charm all of its own. But Matt knew nothing of her thoughts.

'Is that why you won't admit that Steven is Tim's father?' he asked abruptly.

Helen shook her head wearily. 'Please Matt, don't let's go into all that again. I can't take it. Not now. Not at this moment.' And hearing the faint unsteadiness in Helen's voice Matt's eyes softened. He put out one hand and touched her cheek with a gentle finger.

'I'm sorry, Helen. I didn't mean to upset you. God knows you must have had enough problems during the last ten years without my adding to them.'

Helen heard the caressing note in his voice and shivered inwardly. Matt was using his devastating charm again and she seemed to have no defences against it. She stared down at her fingers, linking them tightly in her lap. 'I just don't know what to say,' she whispered. 'There are so many things to consider. I don't know what to do for the best.'

His hands on her shoulders were gentle but firm as he turned her to face him. No one had the right to such beautiful, warm, dark eyes, Helen thought as her own gaze was transfixed by them. 'Trust me, Helen,' he said. 'Believe me, I only have your best interests at heart. Come and live at Ellermere. You won't regret it, I promise you.'

This final plea of Matt's seemed to settle the matter. It was only later, when he had left and Helen had walked into the cottage and closed the door, that she began to wonder if she was going completely mad. When Matt had been next to her, smiling at her, his suggestion had begun to seem like the only logical solution. It was only now when she was alone again that the doubts began to materialise. Going to live at Ellermere was madness. Why had she allowed herself to be persuaded into it? If she could have truly believed that Matt had her best interests at heart maybe she would have been less worried. But despite his kindness to her she couldn't help suspecting his motives. Her thoughts were in a turmoil for the rest of the day.

Tim at least had no such reservations. She told him they were moving when he came home from school and he was, predictably, delighted. 'Great!' he enthused, executing a war dance around the tiny room, whooping crazily. 'We're going to Ellermere! We're going to Ellermere!' he yelled at the top of his voice.

'Pipe down, titch,' Helen said, laughing despite her misgivings as he hugged her tightly. 'Go and wash your hands and face before we have tea.' It was nice to know that one of them was pleased, she thought with a wry grimace as Tim ran off in the direction of the bathroom. Her son didn't see any of the problems they would encounter. Uncle Matt had invited them and that was good enough for him. 'We're only staying until Uncle Phil comes back from Spain,' she told him later, as they washed the dishes after their evening meal.

Tim pulled a face, his bottom lip faintly sulky. 'Do we have to go back to Manchester, Mum? Couldn't we stay in the Lake District for ever?'

'Don't you want to see Uncle Phil again?' Helen asked and Tim nodded.

'Of course I do, but I was just thinking, there would be plenty of room for him to come and stay with us at Ellermere. He'd like Uncle Matt. We could all go out together. That would be great.'

Helen finished the last of the dishes and put them to drain. All the people Tim loved best secure in one place. Helen knew just how he felt and there was a tight, bitter pain in her chest as she replied. 'I'm afraid it's not quite so simple, love. We shall be guests ourselves. We can't just issue invitations to all and sundry.'

'Uncle Matt won't mind,' Tim insisted cheerfully, and Helen left it there. Her son was happy. The unpleasant incidents at school apparently completely forgotten. The problem of Philip could wait, she decided. That was the least of her worries at the moment.

She and Tim spent their entire weekend packing. The bulk of the furniture came with the cottage but they had accumulated a surprising number of possessions during their stay in the cottage and Tim was determined to take everything with him, down to the last conker in his collection. Matt had arranged for a van to call on Monday morning and collect their belongings so on Saturday Mr Williams helped Helen to carry the empty tea chests and cases down from the loft. He was a small, weather-beaten man but his wiry body possessed surprising strength and he manhandled the clumsy boxes with enviable ease.

'Do you want any help with your packing?' he asked when they had finished. They were standing in the middle of the small room surrounded by boxes and tea chests and there was barely space to move in any direction.

'No, it's very kind of you to offer, Mr Williams,' Helen smiled. 'You've been a big help already and I think it all looks a great deal more daunting than it actually is.' He left then with the cheerful direction that she had to give a shout if she needed anything and both she and Tim were hard at work clearing the books from the shelves when Mrs Williams came in at lunchtime.

'I've brought a casserole for your dinner,' she said. 'You carry on with what you're doing. I'll put it in the oven and you can eat when you're ready.'

She bustled into the kitchen and Helen stood and watched her kindly neighbour, feeling very close to tears. Mrs Williams' tall, thin figure seemed to possess a boundless energy and Helen knew she would miss her dreadfully. Mrs Williams came out of the kitchen now, smiling, her cheeks flushed, wiping her hands on the front of her apron. 'That's done,' she said. 'Eat when you and Tim feel like it.'

'It's very kind of you . . .'

'Nonsense, love. We'll do anything we can to help, you know that. We shall miss you, Helen.' Her eyes flew to Tim who was still happily piling books into a packing case and she smiled again. 'You've got a grand boy there. It's been a pleasure to have you both as neighbours.' She hesitated now as though searching carefully for the right words. 'If you need any help at any time.' She paused again, giving Helen a shrewd glance from her kind, grey eyes. 'Help of any kind, don't hesitate to ask, will you, my dear? I know it's not been easy for you and Tim these last weeks, but if things don't work out as you hoped where you're going, Fred and I will be happy to have you stay with us until you've sorted yourselves out. We can't offer you much, but you're welcome to the spare bedroom at any time.'

Helen, not usually the most demonstrative of people, stepped forward instinctively, hugging Mrs Williams tall figure tightly. 'Thank you, you're very kind,' she whispered huskily.

Mrs Williams squeezed Helen's hand. 'Remember, come to us at any time.' She turned then and bustled out, looking ready to burst into tears herself and Helen moved quietly over to the packing case she had been filling before Mrs Williams came in, her head bent, hiding her face from Tim as she wrapped her only decent tea service in tissue paper and placed the pieces carefully into the box. It was a Royal Albert china service which her Aunt Lily had inherited from her own mother and the gold and dark blue of the pattern swam in a hazy blur in front of Helen's tear-filled eyes.

Mrs Williams saw a great deal more than she was saying, Helen realised. She must have heard the gossip about Tim, guessed why they were leaving, but like Helen, had her doubts about Ellermere as a place of refuge. But she was far too kind to pass any judgment on Helen's decision. If everyone in the village had been as tolerant as her neighbour Helen doubted whether she would be leaving now. People could be so cruel, she reflected bitterly. She knew she had been a fool, behaved badly, in the past. But she had only been sixteen when Tim had been conceived. Clearly some people thought she ought to go on paying for her mistake the rest of her life.

'Are you okay, Mum?'

Tim's voice at her side made Helen jump. She had been too intent on her own thoughts to notice his quiet approach. She lifted her head and gave him what she hoped was a warm, confident smile. 'I'm fine,' she murmured. 'A bit sad that's all,' she admitted, ruffling his hair affectionately. 'I shall miss the cottage, and Mr and Mrs Williams.'

'Don't worry, Mum.' Tim was holding her arm, a very adult expression on his face as he sought to reassure her. 'We'll be okay, you'll see. We'll still be together. We'll still have fun.'

Helen stared at her son, her throat constricted with emotion. 'You're right, Tim. Being together, that's the important thing.' She forced a teasing smile, the trembling of her lips so slight that he didn't notice. 'But if you don't hurry up with that tea-chest, you and it will still be here when the rest of the luggage has gone.'

Tim grinned back at her and returned quite happily to the task he was doing. But Helen couldn't erase his words from her head. He was right. She had been weakly bemoaning things she couldn't alter, but really she was incredibly lucky. She had Tim. They were together. Did it matter whether they lived at Fell Cottage or Ellermere? Surely their relationship was the important thing, and it had taken her son, with the clear-sighted view of childhood, to remind her of that fact.

By Sunday evening, to Helen's amazement, the packing was completely finished. She stood in the middle of the living room when Tim had gone to bed, staring about her. Even with a bright fire burning in the grate the cottage looked bleak and shabby. It had been their personal belongings, the books and pictures and brightly coloured cushions which had made the small house into a home and she had to remember that fact.

Perhaps as a result of her more optimistic frame of mind she fell asleep straight away that night and when the alarm bell rang she sprang out of bed immediately, feeling refreshed and invigorated by her dreamless

slumber. She walked over to the window and pulled
back the curtains. The small front garden was shrouded
in mist, the trees below the house almost invisible—
faint shapes, eerie shadows in the thick, grey vapour.
But at least it wasn't raining, Helen reflected as she
pulled on her dressing gown and clattered down the
stairs. She had dreaded moving in the rain. They had
moved into Fell Cottage during a cloudburst. Mud and
water had seeped everywhere. Some of her books still
bore the scars of that experience.

The sun came out as she and Tim were having
breakfast, the mist slowly drifting away, so that when
the removal men arrived the sky was a deep, vivid blue,
reminding Helen painfully of hot summer days she and
Tim had spent at the cottage. She hadn't known
whether to expect Matt or not this morning, but she
told herself now that she was pleased he hadn't come.
The men he had sent were courteous and efficient and
started work immediately, loading boxes on to the van.
Tim was keen to help but Helen realised very quickly
that she was in the way and she strolled off in the
direction of the trees behind the cottage determined to
have one last, sentimental look around before they left.

She wasn't away very long but when she strolled back
the Range Rover was parked alongside the removal van
and Matt himself was standing in front of the cottage
talking to Mrs Williams, Tim at his side, one of Matt's
hands resting on her son's shoulders. Helen stopped
dead, guessing that for one brief instant her own face
had worn the same idiotic expression of pleasure and
excitement that her son's was wearing as he gazed up at
Matt. Certainly that was how she felt inside. Her colour
had risen and her heart was beating ridiculously fast.
Just what had she let herself in for, going to live in the
same house as Matt? If just the sight of him could make

her feel like this, what was living so close to him going to do to her?

She forced herself to start walking again, her stride as carelessly unconcerned as she could make it, hands thrust deep into the pockets of her jeans. They had all seen her now and Tim rushed towards her, totally unselfconscious in his excitement.

'We've been waiting for you, Mum. Uncle Matt's come to take us straight to Ellermere.'

Helen's arm automatically slid around her son's shoulders. She shook her head, feeling the breeze lift her curls, putting up an unsteady hand to brush them back from her forehead. 'I shan't be able to come with you, Tim. There'll be work to done when all the boxes have been taken away. The floors will need sweeping . . .'

'That's all arranged. Mr Jones has agreed to sweep the floors after your luggage has been removed and Mrs Williams tells me she will go in later to make a final check. If anything else needs doing I will send someone down from the house tomorrow.' Matt's deep tones were impossible to ignore and for the first time that morning Helen raised her eyes and allowed herself to really look at him. It was the worst form of self-indulgence but she discovered that it was impossible to prevent it, impossible to turn her gaze away again. He was formally dressed as though ready to leave for work the moment his task of transporting them to Ellermere was done but even his dark business suit, the restrained elegance of pale blue shirt and matching tie couldn't disguise the breadth of his shoulders or the powerful grace of his lean, muscled body.

Her gaze flickered upwards towards his face. He was, she discovered, smiling at her in a way that made her heart tremble. It was a smile as unselfconsciously welcoming as Tim's had been and instinctively Helen shook her head, a final spurt of self-preservation making her say, 'I ought to stay. The cottage is my responsibility after all.'

This time it was Mrs Williams who answered, 'What good would it do, Helen? As Mr Seymour says, I can check around the cottage and make sure that everything is left as it ought to be. No sense you hanging around feeling miserable when it isn't necessary.'

'It's very kind of you,' Helen said and her sigh was barely audible, hidden by her automatic response to Mrs Williams' kind offer. She sensed that further protest would be useless. Mrs Williams clearly wanted to help and it would be churlish to refuse. Besides, where was the point? It was stupid to try and avoid the drive to Ellermere with Matt when, for the next few weeks at least, she and Tim would be living in the same house.

Once her decision was made she pushed any further doubts to the back of her mind. Quickly she ran into the cottage to fetch her jacket and handbag. She didn't linger. The small living room was stripped of everything that had made it home to herself and Tim but when she went back outside Matt and her son were already beside the car, only Mr and Mrs Williams were at the gate waiting to say their farewells. It was a painful moment.

'Come and see us soon, love,' Mr Williams said giving her a quick hug.

Mrs Williams embraced Helen warmly. 'Remember, Helen, if you need it the spare bedroom is always waiting,' she whispered.

'You're very kind. I will remember,' Helen promised, the lump in her throat roughening her tones, her eyes blinded by unshed tears as she climbed into the car. Matt closed the door and walked around to slide into the seat beside her. Both Helen and Tim turned, waving out of the back window as the car began to move away from the cottage. Tim's excitement had suddenly evaporated, Helen realised, looking at his woebegone expression. Two years out of a child's life felt like forever, but she had no words of comfort to offer him at the moment. She was too upset herself. It had been a disturbing morning, for more reasons than one.

As though respecting their need for silence Matt said very little at first and maybe it was his own relaxed attitude but now that Helen was actually in the car with him she no longer felt quite as strained as she had expected to do. Tim was sitting on the back seat, his nose pressed against the window, his warm breath misting the glass, totally preoccupied with his own thoughts and Helen might as well have been alone with Matt.

He had been very kind, she reflected, watching him covertly from the corner of her eye as he handled the powerful car with the smooth economy of movement she had come to expect from him. He needn't have invited Tim and herself to live at Ellermere. It was a big house, of course, but not so vast that two unexpected guests could be accommodated without being noticed. She wondered if he'd considered what their continued presence would mean. She wondered if he'd had second thoughts about inviting them. His offer of a home had been an instinctive one. Was he regretting it now? Her eyelashes flickered upwards as she studied him intently from beneath their dark shadow. And he turned his head at that moment, smiling, as though he knew she had been watching him and was faintly amused, even pleased by it.

'Spring is on the way,' he said, tactfully ignoring her embarrassment, the car slowing as he pointed to the small area of mossy, rock-strewn woodland beside the road. The trees were old ones, their branches straggling untidily, brushing the ground, their buds still showing no sign of green. Helen leaned forward, her cheeks still flushed but her embarrassment temporarily forgotten as she saw the rich carpet of nodding, golden daffodils among the trees.

'Oh Matt, they're beautiful,' she breathed and he nodded, agreeing with her.

'Wordsworth would have been proud of them.'

'Your mother and I walked through the woods to the boathouse last time I was at Ellermere,' she told him, glancing almost shyly at his face. 'The bulbs your father planted were just coming into flower.'

Matt turned his head briefly, smiling at Helen. 'I sometimes think my father missed his true vocation in life by going into the family business. I often wonder if he and Mother would have been far happier running a small nursery somewhere in the country where they could have pottered around outdoors to their hearts' content.'

'Things rarely work out so conveniently,' Helen said with a faint, unconsciously wistful sigh. She knew from her own experience that turning a hobby into a full time job was not only difficult but took away much of the pleasure. 'I suspect that if your parents had needed to make a living from the business they would have had to work far too hard to really enjoy what they were doing.'

Matt's lips twisted into a faint, wry grimace. 'You're probably right,' he agreed, a faint thread of self-contempt colouring his tones. 'Sometimes, Helen, I wonder exactly what you must think of us. We've had success handed to us on a plate, haven't we, the Seymours?' He turned his head, giving her a brief, guarded look. 'Do you despise us for having such an

easy life, when you and your family have had to work
so hard?'

'Of course not,' Helen protested instantly, taken
aback both by his words and the self-derisive way he
uttered them. 'You work hard, Matt. You always have
done. I think you would have made a success of life if
your parents had never had a penny.'

'A success of life! I wonder? How does one measure
success, Helen? Because I'm damned if I know. Is it
measured in happiness, or money, or in the ability to
form and sustain a close relationship? Because taking at
least two out of three of those criteria into account, I
have failed miserably.'

Helen shook her head unhappily. She didn't quite
know how the conversation had taken this twist but she
suspected it was all her own fault and she had
discovered during the last few minutes that she hated to
see that bitter, self-derisive twist to Matt's lips,
transforming his features. She put out a tentative hand
and touched his sleeve. 'I'm sorry if I said something to
upset you. I didn't mean to criticise you, honestly.'

He shook his head, turning to smile at her once again
and if the smile didn't quite reach his eyes, Helen tried
not to notice. 'You said nothing, Helen, believe me.
Let's forget it, shall we?' And then after a moment as
though deliberately shaking off his mood of introspection, 'Look, through the trees you can just see the roof
of Ellermere.'

Tim bounced forward, coming suddenly to life, his
elbows on the back of Matt's seat. 'Where? I can't see
it. Point to it again, Uncle Matt,' he cried.

Helen was content to sit quietly after that, their
approach to Ellermere punctuated by Tim's excited
cries, his misery at leaving Fell Cottage apparently
completely forgotten. How odd life was, Helen

reflected, watching the play of emotions across her son's excited face. The last months had been so unreal that she still sometimes wondered if it was all a dream. Would she awaken one morning and find that she and Tim were back at Fell Cottage and things were as they had always been. But no, Matt and his family had made far too much of an impact on her life for them to be anything but solid flesh and blood and Ellermere itself was very much a part of the present, she reflected as Matt drew the car to a gentle halt in front of its elegant, sprawling façade. Mrs Seymour was already at the door, smiling, the gaunt lines of her face transformed with pleasure as she returned Tim's excited little wave. Tim jumped out of the car the moment it stopped, running up the steps between the stone lions straight into Mrs Seymour's waiting arms. Helen watched them both turn and walk into the house feeling an unaccountably large lump in her throat.

'My mother is very pleased that you've agreed to stay with us.' Helen became aware that Matt had turned towards her, one arm resting casually along the back of her seat, his eyes on her face. She dropped her head, fixing her gaze on her slender fingers discovering that she was not yet quite so comfortable in Matt's company that she could meet his eyes without effort.

'It's kind of you to say so,' she murmured. 'But I can't help feeling guilty. Have you really considered what our living here will mean? The arrangements were made in such a hurry. There was no time to think things through properly. Tim is a normal, healthy boy. He usually behaves well, but he's no angel. He's often noisy and always very untidy . . .'

'Listen to me very carefully, Helen,' Matt replied. He was watching her steadily, holding her gaze, his eyes seeming to tell her something of far more significance than the quiet, reassuring words he uttered. 'I have no doubts. Ellermere is your home, both yours and Tim's. You will always be welcome here. And we hope, all of us, that you will never think of leaving again!'

CHAPTER NINE

HELEN stood gazing down at the dew-wet gardens below her window, Philip's letter still clutched in one shaking hand. How was it possible for so many weeks to have passed with such terrifying speed? April ... May, the months had disappeared as though they were merely hours or minutes. Already the early roses were flowering in Madeline Seymour's garden. Summer was almost upon them. Philip's letter informing her of his arrival in England ought not to have been unexpected, and yet it had been. Both unexpected and unwelcome. There was no point in trying to fool herself about that. She had hidden the truth too long, Helen realised. Far too long! These last weeks she had drifted through life conveniently forgetting all the things she ought to have remembered. There had been stern resolutions made before she moved into Ellermere but she had ignored every one. She had been living in a dream world. It had taken Philip's letter to bring her back to reality.

A faint breeze drifted in from the garden gently wafting the silky, blue curtains away from the window, rustling the pages of the letter in her hand. Helen glanced down at it again. Philip's elegant script was very distinctive, strong, flowing strokes which refused to allow her to bury her head in the sand any longer.

'I know how desperate you must have been to accept help from the Seymours,' he had written. 'I can imagine how unhappy, how uncomfortable you must feel, living in that house again ...'

Helen's lips twisted into a faint travesty of a smile as

148

she read these words. If only Philip knew! She had never been so happy in her life before, living with a man she ought to hate and fear, seeing him every day. She simply hadn't realised the fact before. It was Philip's letter that had pulled the veil back from her eyes so that at last she could see things as they really were. How could she have let it happen? How could she have allowed herself to fall in love with Matt again? For that was what had happened, she acknowledged with painful honesty. The symptoms were unmistakable and yet, until this morning she had failed to recognise them.

'You fool! You crazy fool!' She bent her head, one shaking hand pressed to her eyes. There had been quiet desperation in the few faintly muttered words, and that was exactly how she felt—desperate—wondering why it had taken her so long to realise what was happening. She had enjoyed Matt's company so much, surely that in itself ought to have warned her. But no, because she had fallen in love with him before and suffered the consequences, she had thought that she was safe. Forewarned is forearmed, that was the way she had reasoned. She couldn't be such an idiot as to allow history to repeat itself. She knew Matt had loved Natalie very deeply. She guessed that he loved her still. Her name was never mentioned at Ellermere, not by anyone. Helen sensed that the subject was still too painful for discussion and she had never quite had the courage to broach it herself. She saw now that her own reluctance ought to have been an additional warning. She had been avoiding the issue, not only because she feared to hurt Matt, but because she had been unwilling to have her fears confirmed.

But it hadn't been entirely her own fault, she realised. The days had passed so peacefully she had been lulled into a false sense of security. It was with a feeling of incredulity that Helen looked back now and saw just how much of her free time she had spent with Matt. The long walks over the fells with Tim and Katy had become a Sunday ritual. Even on wet days they had set out early in the morning, wrapped in cagoules and waterproof trousers, Tim insisting on taking turns with Matt to carry the rucksack containing their sandwiches. But the warm, sunny days had been the best. Rising early, breakfasting with just Matt and the children. Was that where love had happened, Helen wondered, out on the open fells with no sound to disturb them but the bleating of the sturdy mountain sheep or the occasional curlew calling as it flew above them.

Or had it happened at Ellermere during the long firelit evenings they had shared with Mrs Seymour? They had talked about everything under the sun. It was amazing the number of interests they had in common— the books they had both read, the music they both enjoyed listening to. They had led a surprisingly quiet, uneventful life. 'I'm afraid you may be a little bored with us, Helen,' Madeline Seymour had said on that first evening. 'Since George died I rarely entertain. Just the occasional business associate of Matt's . . . a few old friends.' But Helen hadn't been bored. She had enjoyed the close family atmosphere at Ellermere, enjoyed simply being with Matt. Although she had rarely been alone with him. Sometimes Helen had suspected that Matt deliberately avoided that state of affairs. There had certainly never been any romantic togetherness in the moonlight. Perhaps it would have been better for her if there had. Maybe that would have warned her she was in danger of falling in love again.

But then, who could tell when the first seed of love had been planted? Maybe it had started on that very first evening when Matt had come blundering through the snow to Fell Cottage carrying Katy in his arms. Maybe she had always loved him, never stopped. Perhaps that was why she had been so unwilling to admit him into their lives again. She had been afraid—not for Tim's sake, as she had always pretended—but for her own. And she had been right to fear him. She had tried to hold him at arm's length but very slowly, like ivy growing over a tree, one tiny, green shoot imperceptibly following another, he had forced her to accept him until eventually he had become indispensable to her happiness.

No! No! Helen closed her eyes tightly, her hands clenched into fists at her sides. She refused to indulge in such thoughts. No one person was indispensable to another. She knew her Aunt Lily would have told her that. Human beings were social animals, it was true. But in the last resort everyone was responsible for their own destiny. Matt had only become such an important part of her life because she had allowed him to do so. She had left Ellermere once, and maybe it had been a slow and painful process, but she had forgotten him at last. She would do so again.

'We must leave and go to Philip immediately.' She was halfway across the room before the words had left her lips, the skirt of her cotton dress swinging wildly around her bare legs. She knew they had no choice except to leave, because how could she possibly stay knowing she loved Matt and knowing equally well that he could never return that love. She had too much pride to linger once she had recognised the state of her own feelings. He must never guess what had happened to her. He would pity her and that would be harder to bear than anything. She crossed the room quickly, pausing at the door, turning to look back for a moment, her eyes betraying her sadness.

Matt had chosen these rooms for her. She could still remember the pleasure she had tried so hard to hide when he had shown her around them, how she had protested.

'Don't be an idiot, Helen,' he had said, smiling that familiar, charming smile of his, his eyes crinkling so attractively at the corners. 'The sitting room is ideal for your painting. The light in here is terrific. And no one else is using the place.'

It was the main guest suite. Somewhere that in the past Helen had only peeped into nervously when she knew no one could see her. She hadn't continued her protests very long, and when Matt had left her she had wandered around the rooms feeling curiously light-headed and carefree. She loved beautiful things and the highly polished furniture in her suite was some of the best in the house. She knew enough about antiques to recognise that the elegant chairs beneath the windows were Chippendale; the small table in the corner was French, very delicate, very beautiful. The carpets were a rich blue, their pile thick and luxurious beneath her feet. There were cream and blue curtains at all the windows, the darkest corners of the sitting room brightened by sweetly smelling bowls of daffodils, their pale, creamy petals only one shade deeper that the upholstery on the large, comfortable sofa and chairs. Perhaps the unaccustomed luxury had gone to her head a little because she had buried any doubts, telling herself that for once in her life surely she deserved some comfort. Surely she deserved the chance to relax a little. She had worked hard enough. It couldn't be wrong to enjoy what fate had sent her, not just for a short time, could it?

Helen shook her head, coming back to the present with a deep sigh. Of course it had been wrong. Not only wrong but extremely foolish. It had been a kind of surrender. The first step on the dangerous road to love. She left the room, closing the door quietly behind her. As she descended the stairs she could hear the sound of a vacuum cleaner behind the partly closed door of the drawing room but the hallway was empty and she walked through it quickly, her heels making sharp little sounds on the polished surface of the parquet floor. She knew that Matt was expecting his accountants later in the morning but if she was lucky he would still be in his office, and alone. She had to tell him of her decision to leave, immediately. Before the pain and fear and tension had chance to build up inside her. Telling herself yet again that whatever happened she mustn't allow Matt to realise how she felt about him. It was unpleasant enough to know that she was weak and foolish. But at least her pride was intact. Matt must never guess the truth.

The door to Matt's office was closed but Helen knocked quickly before she could change her mind and almost immediately Matt's quiet voice told her to enter. She pushed open the door, noting without surprise that her fingers were shaking slightly. Her eyes flickered around the room, seeing Matt almost immediately, although he wasn't sitting at his desk as she had half expected but standing by the window, his back to the door gazing out in apparent abstraction. He looked very tired, Helen thought, a distinct sag to those broad shoulders and stupidly her heart went out to him. She felt a tremendous urge to rush across the room and slide her arms around him, lay her head against his broad back. But then he turned abruptly and the moment was gone. If there were shadows on his face Helen told herself they were drawn there by the sun shafting through the tall windows. She was a fool to feel

sorry for him. She needed all her sympathy for herself
this morning.

'Ah, Helen, come and sit down,' he said pointing to
the deep leather chair beside his desk. He smiled but she
could see no warmth in the faint movement of his lips.
She sat down quickly, feeling suddenly more nervous
and miserable than ever. He didn't look even faintly
surprised to see her and yet she had never been to his
office uninvited before. It was very much his private
sanctum, the walls lined with books, the furniture dark
and businesslike. When Helen had been in the room
before papers were strewn on his desk and piled on the
floor beside it, but today everything had been tidied
away, the polished surface was bare, apart from a white
blotter and a small silver dish containing an assortment
of pens and pencils.

He had taken a seat behind the desk and was moving
his chair idly from side to side, watching her. Helen
could feel her knees shaking and hoped he hadn't
noticed. Dear God, this was awful! She didn't know
why but suddenly she felt as though they were complete
strangers. She raised her head, forcing a smile to her
tremulous lips.

'Are you very busy this morning? Can you spare me a
few minutes?' she asked.

His mouth indented in a faint, impersonal smile. 'Of
course, I'm not expecting my accountants until ten-
thirty. I'm free until then,' he added coolly, almost as
though he knew exactly what she had come to tell him
and was determined not to give her any help.

'This is very difficult. I don't know where to begin,'
Helen said shakily.

He leaned forward slightly, the chair creaking as he
did so. 'Is there some problem with your room? Have
you a complaint to make . . .?'

Helen shook her head quickly. 'No, no, of course not. How could I have any complaint? You've all been so kind.' Was it her? she wondered desperately. Was she so uptight, so aware of her feelings for Matt that she was imagining his strange manner? Or was he really behaving as coldly as she thought? Apparently determined to put her on the defensive before she even began. He was watching her now with what Helen felt to be the cool disinterest of a perfect stranger, his face smooth, without expression, telling her nothing.

'I'm glad you are happy with us, Helen,' he replied steadily.

She lowered her eyes, biting her lip in agitation. 'We have been happy, very happy,' she whispered. It was suddenly impossible for her to continue. She stared at the plain brown carpet in silent agony, the words she had planned to say to him sticking in her throat.

'I'm relieved it hear it,' Matt said now. 'For a moment, this morning I thought you had come to tell me you were leaving us.' His voice was quiet and even paced but Helen sensed the control he was exerting to maintain that outward calm, and temporarily at least, she discovered that her own control had deserted her. She raised her head slowly, brushing back the curls from her forehead in a small, unconscious gesture. She had been right. From the moment she had walked into the room he had known what she wanted to say to him and he had been deliberately making it difficult for her.

'You ... you saw the letter,' she faltered and he nodded abruptly, his expression grim.

'Did you think that I wouldn't notice it, Helen? Your friend certainly seems to have intended me to do so. Philip Ackroyd, 473 Victoria Road, Manchester. Wasn't that the address on the back of the envelope?'

Maybe Helen's imagination was working overtime

but the whole cast of his features seemed to have altered since yesterday, the smooth sweep of his bones jutting in sharper outline, his mouth and jaw tight, the dark horizontals of brow and eye cut deeper into his face.

'You knew we would have to leave sometime,' she whispered.

'Did I, Helen?' He shrugged, a barely perceptible movement of his broad shoulders. 'Well, since you say so I suppose I must have known.' He continued to stare at her, his eyes darkly brooding as they rested on her troubled features. 'So ... just when were you planning to leave? How quickly does Philip Ackroyd expect you to come flying back into his arms?'

'It isn't like that,' Helen protested helplessly and Matt raised his dark brows in harsh interrogation.

'No, then explain to me, if you will, just exactly what it is like? Because at the moment I'm finding the situation very difficult to understand. You say you are happy here with us. Tim certainly seems to be so and yet the moment this ... this friend of yours raises his little finger you go rushing back to him.'

Helen bit her lip, knowing she dare not even try to explain. He was very angry with her now, and that hurt, but if he should guess the truth that would be even more painful for her to bear. 'Please Matt,' she whispered. 'You said we could go when Philip returned.'

Matt's lips had twisted into a painful smile. 'So I did! Go, and I shan't try to stop you. Weren't those the platitudes I mouthed? God help me, I meant them too, at the time. Fool that I was I thought it was a safe enough promise to make. I was so sure that once you had lived at Ellermere for a while Philip Ackroyd's charms would be forgotten. Until this morning, until you actually walked into my office, I still believed you would stay with us. It can't have escaped your notice that over the last months we have become very ... fond of you and Tim. And God damn it, Helen!' he exclaimed, his voice rising in angry frustration. 'You have lived in this house for almost three months. I've seen you constantly. Never once in my hearing have you mentioned this man's name. Never once have you given any indication that you care for him. What are you trying to do to me, Helen? Just what am I supposed to think?'

Shakily Helen pushed herself to her feet, her fingers gripping tightly to the back of her chair. She had barely listened to the angry words he hurled at her. The bitter, contemptuous tone was enough, more than enough. She clung trembling to the back of the chair. 'It's no use. I've made up my mind. You've been very kind. I want to thank ...' She stopped abruptly, unable to go on, the words locked painfully inside her. 'Goodbye, Matt,' she whispered. And then, before her control gave way completely she turned and stumbled blindly across the room towards the door while Matt sat and watched her in frozen silence. Only as the door closed firmly behind her did he move and then he groaned aloud.

'God damn it! God damn it to hell!' he said, bending his head, his bare fist thudding so violently on to the top of the desk that one of the pens jumped out of the silver dish and rolled slowly across the polished surface falling unheeded on to the carpet at Matt's feet.

Strangely, when Helen reached her room she didn't cry. She felt beyond tears. Cold, completely dead inside. She refused to think about Matt any longer. She wouldn't remember the cruel things he had said to her or the contemptuous way he said them. He was angry and hurt. He thought she was ungrateful, throwing his kindness back in his face. He simply didn't understand,

and she couldn't explain to him. Even so she thought he could have shown a little more tolerance, a little more compassion. They had become good friends. Surely he ought to realise that if she was leaving her reasons had to be good ones. From the moment she entered his office his behaviour had been unreasonable. He was possessive about Tim, of course, But even so . . .

She sighed heavily, shying away from her thoughts, taking refuge in activity as her Aunt Lily had taught her.

'Don't sit and brood, Helen. Go and clean the windows if you've nothing better to do with yourself.' Hard work had been Aunt Lily's universal panacea. Worries of any sort, headaches, toothache, even influenza, had succumbed to it. Aunt Lily had never taken to bed with any but the most serious illness. 'I shall be all right in a jiffy. I'll work it off,' had been her accustomed cry and now Helen hauled out her shabby suitcases from the bottom of the wardrobe and proceeded to pack them with almost feverish haste. It wasn't necessary. She knew they couldn't leave Ellermere until Monday at the earliest. But she daren't relax, start to think again.

She went to Tim's room and half-emptied his wardrobe. She didn't need a crystal ball to guess his reaction to her news. This old house had become his home. He loved every inch of it. But she couldn't allow herself to be influenced by that fact. She folded jeans and sweaters and placed them carefully on the steadily growing pile in her suitcase. Tim would become accustomed to the idea of living in Manchester, just as she would herself. He loved Philip. There were pluses and minuses to this move. They would cancel each other out in the end. Even to herself these arguments sounded far from convincing but she carried on working doggedly, still fighting the ceaseless battle inside her own head.

By lunchtime all the items she didn't think they would need during the next few days were packed. Helen's head was throbbing. She felt hot and sticky and food was the last thing on her mind at the moment. No doubt Matt would invite his business associates to stay for lunch and the thought of sitting in the dining room, enduring Matt's contemptuous glances and having to make polite conversation caused Helen to shudder. She would skip lunch today and apologise to Mrs Ellis later. Matt would realise why she hadn't put in an appearance and no doubt make some sort of an excuse for her.

She walked over to the window, staring restlessly out into the garden. No wonder she felt hot and uncomfortable. The clear blue sky had clouded over, there was a faintly yellow, sulphurous cast to it now, as though a storm was building up around the lake. The atmosphere was threatening and humid. She was a fool to have done all her packing at once as she had. For one thing Tim would realise as soon as he came home from school that his clothes had disappeared. She wouldn't be able to delay telling him they were moving to Manchester. But after all there was no point in putting off the unpleasant moment, she thought with a sigh. It was best to get the bad news told quickly. But she was a coward, she realised. She didn't want to tell him, not today, not ever. For the first time in her life she was really afraid of her son's reaction. He wouldn't see the need to move, any more than Matt did. She loved Tim. He was all she had. She dreaded the idea that he would look at her with the same bitter contempt she had seen in his father's eyes.

The steadily darkening clouds were increasing, seeming to press down over the landscape, intensifying

the tension in Helen's head and when the first drops of
rain splashed on to the ground it was a welcome release,
galvanising her into instant action as she rushed around
closing the windows tightly. By the time she had
fastened the final catch the rain was lashing down in a
torrent. She stood with her forehead pressed against the
cool glass thinking how refreshing it would be to walk
outside and simply stand there letting the falling water
wash over her, cooling her overheated body. It was only
the thought of Mrs Seymour's horror if she was seen
that stopped her. She had enough explaining to do to
Madeline Seymour without adding to her problems.

The rain hurled itself against the windows in
powerful gusts, almost as though the elements
themselves were angry, trying to punish her, throwing
handfuls of tiny pebbles at the glass like a small child in
a tantrum. Helen didn't retreat. On the contrary she
stood with her eyes riveted on the fierce battle raging
beyond the window. The storm was a fitting culmination
to the events of the morning. Thunder rumbled in the
distance. The wind lashed the branches of the trees into
a frenzy as jagged lightning flashed across the sky.

Helen was so completely absorbed by the spectacle
that she didn't even hear Matt knocking at the door
behind her. She didn't hear him crossing the floor, his
footsteps muffled by the luxurious carpet. His hands
were actually on her shoulders turning her to face him
before she realised he was in the room with her. It was a
shock to swing round and gaze straight into his face.
His eyes were the only alive things in it. They glittered,
feverishly bright, as she was sure her own must do.
There was something unreal about the moment, as
though they were both frozen images on a photograph.
Neither of them moved, neither spoke. They just stared
into each other's eyes as though mesmerised. The storm

was increasing in frenzy, thunder rumbled, lightning cracked. Matt shook his head at last, looking as dazed as Helen herself.

'Are you okay?' he asked, shaking her very gently, and he had to repeat the question before she was able to answer him.

'Yes, yes, of course I am,' she faltered at last. But she felt stunned. Almost as though she had indeed been out in the garden, battered to the ground by the deluge.

'You didn't come down to lunch and my mother was worried.'

'I wasn't hungry ... I'm sorry, I never thought. Tell your mother I didn't mean to worry her.'

The room was dark, its beauty dimmed by the raging storm. Matt's skin looked sickly, pallid in the half light and Helen was possessed of the most ridiculous, weak-kneed urge to throw her arms around his neck and cling to him. 'Do you love me, Matt?' she would cry. 'Because I love you! I've loved you always. I don't think I will ever stop.' But she knew she couldn't say it and she shivered standing there with Matt's fingers on her bare shoulders. She was mad to even let such thoughts enter her head. Matt had been her friend in the past but that was over now. He didn't even desire her any longer. It was months since he had kissed her and then it had been meant as a punishment rather than a demonstration of passion. He had made no secret of that.

'Helen, for God's sake, what's the matter with you? Are you ill? Shall I call the doctor?'

Helen blinked, her dark lashes fluttering. She had been standing blank-eyed staring into Matt's face, her thoughts miles away. No wonder Matt was looking at her with such a worried frown. He must think that the storm had turned her brain. She pressed one hand to her forehead. 'I'm sorry, I have a headache, that's all. I meant to lie down and try to sleep but the storm disturbed me.'

'I think you had better lie down anyway,' Matt told her grimly. He was already urging her towards the bedroom, one hand on her elbow and Helen had no choice but to go with him. Why, oh why did he have to come to her room so unexpectedly? She had had no time to school herself for this meeting. Her defences were dangerously low, her mind and senses both reeling crazily. She was scared even to open her mouth in case she somehow revealed what she was thinking. She daren't meet his eyes. She knew her own expression would be far too easy to read.

Matt was still holding her arm in his grasp. 'Lie down, Helen, before you fall down,' he instructed brusquely when they reached the bedroom and she did as she was told, flopping back helplessly on top of the blue and cream duvet cover. She couldn't tell whether Matt was still angry with her. His tone was curt but there was an underlying gentleness in his voice which confused her. He had been in the bathroom but was walking back towards her now and she closed her eyes tightly. It was a very inadequate form of defence, she realised. The ostrich syndrome, burying her head in the sand, trying to be invisible.

The bed creaked as he lowered his weight on to it and she felt the touch of a cool, damp cloth on her brow. 'How does that feel?' he asked quietly.

'It feels good,' she whispered through dry lips. She wished she couldn't hear that thread of concern in his voice. She wished he wouldn't be so kind to her. She was afraid that very soon, if he didn't leave, her tears were going to mingle with the cool drops of moisture trickling down her cheeks from the cloth on her forehead.

He was still there, staring down at her. 'Shall I fetch you something to eat in your room?'

Helen shook her head restlessly. 'No, no, I'm fine,' she insisted, feeling her stomach muscles tighten at his continued presence. Just go away, she wanted to cry. Leave me alone!

'A cup of coffee then?'

'Nothing, honestly!' Helen protested.

Still he didn't get up and leave as she wanted him to do. He sat quietly for another moment, still watching her, and then: 'I'm sorry, Helen,' he sighed. 'I'm afraid this is all my fault. I don't know what got into me this morning. I behaved like a monster. I didn't mean to lose my temper,' he added softly. 'In my own mind I had the interview mapped out before you even came into the room. I was going to be cool and calm. Persuade you to stay by parading a whole lot of reasoned arguments in front of you. I don't quite know what happened but my reasoned arguments seemed to fly out of the window fairly quickly. But they are still there, in my head, waiting to be said. In fact there's so much I want to say to you I hardly know where to begin. I've waited, giving you the time I thought you needed and now I'm afraid I may have left it too late. But I have to try, Helen. Will you listen to what I have to say?'

At some point during the conversation Matt had picked up one of Helen's hands, his thumb massaging her palm, stroking it almost absent-mindedly as though she was a stray kitten needing the warmth of human contact. Helen knew she ought to pull her hand out of his clasp but for some reason she hadn't done so and now the slow, rhythmic movement of his thumb against her palm, his voice, its tone deep and faintly husky, both combined to cast a spell over Helen. She was barely

listening to his words, instead she was drowning in
sensation, her whole body tinglingly aware of Matt
sitting only inches away from her on the bed. She was
imagining the caressing note in his voice, of course and
the faint tremble in the lean fingers which held her own.
But where was the harm in letting him touch her like
this? Very soon she would have disappeared from his
life forever. Surely for a short time she could pretend
that her dreams had become reality, she could pretend
that this moment would go on for ever.

He hadn't spoken again and slowly she opened her
eyes, her stomach giving a crazy lurch of excitement. He
was staring down at her mouth as though mesmerised
by the soft, trembling curve of it and Helen could feel
the slow tremble which had begun in her stomach
spread to every inch of her body. 'I thought you hated
me,' she whispered as he drew her captive hand towards
his lips, kissing each slender finger very gently in turn.

'Dear God, Helen, sometimes I wish that I did.'

He was staring down at her and Helen could feel her
bones melting under the intensity of that look. 'I don't
want you to hate me,' she whispered.

'Don't talk,' he commanded, and very slowly his
mouth began its tormenting descent towards her own.

Helen knew that this was the moment when she
ought to stop him. Tell him to leave her alone. Beat on
his chest with her fists if necessary but even as the
thought came into her head she had thrown the cloth
off her forehead and her arms were curving possessively
around his neck, the dark, silky hair so like her son's
caressing her bare skin, sending tiny shivers of
excitement along her veins.

'Helen, darling,' Matt cried and swiftly his head
covered the tiny space between them, his lips claiming
hers with hungry insistence. And only now did Helen

realise that for weeks she had been waiting for this, craving for him to kiss her. Perhaps later she would regret the unthinking sensuality of her actions, but now all she could remember was that she loved him. Sanity had departed the minute he had looked at her with such pasionate, pleading eyes.

He was kissing her neck now, his tongue sliding along her white skin as though he would like to devour every inch of her. He kissed her eyes, the delicate curve of cheek and jawline, his hands moving over her body with restless, seeking urgency, like a blind man having to feel his way and Helen moaned and twisted beneath him, her breath coming in ragged, jerky sobs. Her dress fastened with a row of tiny, white buttons down the front and he undid them all, one by one, with tormenting slowness. Helen lifted her heavy lids and he was watching her, his eyes dark, glittering with desire.

'Beautiful,' he breathed, staring down as he parted her bodice, very gently touching the soft, white skin of one throbbing breast. He bent his head, taking her swollen nipple in his mouth, teasing it gently with his teeth so that Helen cried aloud, pressing herself against him in mindless passion. 'I want you,' he groaned, his mouth against her breast and Helen answered:

'Yes!' The word coming out thickly, as though her lips and tongue were swollen. Her whole body was on fire from his touch. Her hands slid beneath his shirt, touching the skin of his back, pressing her palms against his damp flesh, feeling the same, fierce, throbbing heat devouring him, and glorying in it. At this moment her body belonged, not to her, but to a sensual, abandoned stranger who responded to Matt's passionate lovemaking with an almost animal excitement.

When he left her briefly to tear off his own clothes

she allowed her eyes to linger on the perfection of his naked body without shame. She reached out instinctively and slid her hands over his firm, warm chest feeling the ripple of bone and muscle beneath her fingers, enjoying the shudder of pleasure that ran through him at her touch. He stared down at her, his eyes seeming to burn her tender skin with their fierce gaze.

'I won't share you, Helen,' he whispered deeply. 'Not with Philip Ackroyd, not with anyone. I want all of you. No secrets. No pretence. Say that you'll stay at Ellermere with me. Forget the past.'

Helen trembled in his embrace, the colour draining out of her cheeks leaving her pale and waxen. Her brief escape from reality had passed, she realised despairingly. He wanted her, he said. Why then had he not just gone ahead and made love to her? Why did he have to spoil the moment with words? Why did there have to be questions and conditions? He had made her think again. He had broken the spell—made her remember that he had never once said he loved her.

She closed her eyes, trying once again to capture the magic, the excitement that had flared between them, knowing instinctively that already it was too late. Why, when she had been willing to surrender her body without protest, could she not say the few words he wanted to hear?

'I can't. I just can't!' And only when she opened her eyes and saw the expression on Matt's face did she realise that she had groaned the words aloud.

Matt's hand slid trembling over her white throat as though he didn't know whether to caress her tender skin or choke the life out of her. 'Why, Helen? Why? Does what has just happened between us mean nothing to you?' he cried, his voice hoarse with shocked emotion.

Helen moved her head despairingly from side to side, strands of soft hair clinging to her cheeks and damp forehead. 'Don't, Matt, please,' she whispered. 'I can't explain.'

He stared down at her, dawning anger replacing the anguish in his eyes. 'You still intend to live with Philip Ackroyd?' he asked.

The urge to explain everything had never been so strong. Helen's lips actually parted to utter the betraying words, but Matt didn't allow her to speak. 'If you love Philip Ackroyd so damned much what the hell are you doing here, half naked in my arms? You would have let me make love to you. You wanted me, I'll swear you did. You had no intention of stopping me.'

The torrent of contemptuous words effectively silenced any explanation that Helen had been tempted to make. Looking at his harsh, condemnatory expression she knew it would have been useless. He wouldn't believe her. And maybe it was better this way. One explanation would inevitably lead to another. In the end she would find herself admitting that she loved him. She had left her body without defences today but her mind was still her own. If she once told him of her love she would have given him everything—her past, her present and her future. There would be nowhere to hide. She would be totally exposed and defenceless.

'I never thought I would hear myself saying this to you,' Matt continued hoarsely. 'But you're just a weak, immoral little bitch and maybe you and Philip Ackroyd deserve each other after all. God!' He threw back his head, the laugh he gave a low, bitter denunciation. 'When I think how I blamed Steven for taking your innocence. I actually hated my own brother for a while.'

'Matt, please,' Helen begged, knowing the brief idyll was over, yet still not completely able to accept it.

He shook his head fiercely, pushing himself to his feet, staring down at her slender body, the white breasts, the abandoned posture of her sprawling limbs outlined against the quilt, forcing himself to ignore its seductive attraction. He reached for his clothes, pulling them on with almost feverish haste. 'No, Helen, I'm not going to touch you again. It's finished! God knows, I wanted to make love to you but maybe it's as well things turned out as they did. I surely don't want another Seymour bastard on my conscience. Believe me, one is enough.' He hurled the words at her as though they were missiles designed to hurt her as he had been hurt. 'Go to Philip Ackroyd! Give him your love but don't expect me to wish you joy.'

Helen watched in silence, unable to move a muscle as he turned and walked across the room. He closed the door without looking in her direction again and only then did she move, burying her head in the pillow, sobbing as though her heart would break. She felt no sense of shame for the way she had responded to Matt. Perhaps others would have condemned the fact that for the second time in her life she had succumbed to his lovemaking but she knew she would have given herself freely, without restraint, without regrets. Her tears were not for that.

She wept for the false pride which had prevented her from admitting the truth to him. She cried for the stubbornness in her soul which wouldn't allow her to say, I love you, unless he said it first. Maybe Matt had cared for her a little but now she would never know. If he ever thought of her in the future it would be with contempt and Helen prayed for the strength to carry that knowledge with her, bravely, into the lonely future.

CHAPTER TEN

IT was hot. For five whole weeks the entire country had slowly frazzled under a burning sun. Helen could feel the sweat trickling down the hollow between her breasts and she suspected that her white T-shirt would be clinging damply to her back where she had leaned against the seat of the coach. Every window had been wide open but even on the relatively quiet stretches of road where the driver had been able to pick up speed the cooler air coming in at the windows had been minimal. Helen had realised the moment she and Tim climbed on to the coach what a stupid idea the outing had been. But Manchester was like an oven. She had craved the sight of green fields, wooded valleys and hills empty of people. In fact Lyme Park had been almost as crowded as the city. They had eaten their picnic a couple of metres from a family whose idea of a day out was to lounge in the sun, beer cans and sweet packets scattered around them, listening to Radio One.

No, it hadn't been a success, Helen reflected bitterly, looking ahead to where Tim was slouching along in front of her. He had discovered a rusting iron bar and he was running it over the wall, his hands and the sides of his jeans already covered in dark reddish-brown powder. But Helen hadn't the heart to stop him. In the last months he had turned from a cheerful, considerate boy into an unhappy, often uncooperative stranger and she knew it was her own fault. What could she say to him when she knew exactly how he was feeling? Moving to Manchester after the beauty and freedom of the Lakes, who could blame him for trying to rebel?

Maybe if Philip had lived in one of the lusher suburbs it would have been easier to adjust, but his had been an inner city parish. The work had often been thankless and unrewarding but he had made some good friends, and he had been needed. Consequently, when he bought his own house on retirement it had been within walking distance of his old church. The area as a place to live left a great deal to be desired, Helen conceded, looking around her now with critical eyes. Litter was one of the minor problems and today with most of the shops closed, the streets looked drabber and dirtier than ever.

She quickened her step, anxious to catch up with Tim, unwilling to encourage this mood of introspection. It was futile and dangerous to allow her thoughts free rein. She had learned that the hard way over the last bitter weeks. Pride was a poor substitute for love, she had found. And if it had not been for the fact that she remembered Matt's contemptuous parting words all too clearly and knew he wouldn't want to see her again, she would have run to Ellermere and begged him to take them back, whatever his conditions. But it was impossible, and the knowledge that she had destroyed Tim's happiness as well as her own was an additional torment to disturb her in the dark, lonely nights, when sleep was only possible if she unwillingly swallowed the pills her doctor had prescribed for her.

Tim turned the corner into Victoria Road just ahead of her. He had dropped the rusty bar, rubbing his hands on the front of his T-shirt and he looked down unhappily now as Helen caught up with him. 'Sorry, Mum,' he mumbled in half-reluctant apology. 'I didn't realise it was so dirty.'

'Don't worry, love, it will wash.' Helen smiled,

ruffling his hair with reassuring fingers. 'Look,' she raised her arm and pointed down the street to where a thin, brown-haired boy about the same size as Tim was standing staring in their direction, 'that's David, isn't it? And he looks as though he's coming to meet you.'

Tim waved to his friend, his face breaking into its old, infectious grin as he ran off towards him. Helen heaved a sigh of relief. Thank goodness for David Barnes and his mother. David was a year older than Tim and the one bright spot in his existence at the moment. Molly, his mother, was separated from her husband and she and Helen had become firm friends since they had moved in with Philip. Helen could see her standing at the gate now, tall and dark with a warm, healthy tan, she waved as cheerfully as her son had done, smiling at Helen as she approached.

'Hi! How did it go? Did you enjoy the break?'

Helen pulled a small face. 'It was hot and dusty and overcrowded,' and then with a reluctant grin, 'but otherwise, yes, it was wonderful. Tim tore his best jeans trying to climb a tree and then, when I went to buy some ice-creams he wandered off so that by the time I'd found him again the blessed things had melted.'

Molly laughed, shaking her head. 'You had a marvellous time I can tell. And believe me, Helen, it shows.'

Helen grimaced ruefully. 'Thanks a million, friend.'

Molly laughed again, but reluctantly. 'Honestly, Helen, you are an idiot. You look about as lively as a wet dish cloth at the moment, and you know what the doctor said.'

Helen shook her head quickly, frowning in her son's direction.

'He hasn't heard,' Molly assured her, following the direction of Helen's eyes. The two boys had a small army of tanks and trucks on the garden wall and were loudly firing matchstick cannonballs in each other's direction. 'But if you're not careful you will crack up completely and you certainly won't be much use to Tim in hospital,' she added sternly, and then after a moment, 'Look, I was thinking of taking David to the swimming baths. Why don't you let Tim come with us? It would be company for David. Tim would enjoy it and you could put your feet up for a couple of hours.'

It sounded like a wonderful idea but as Helen suspected that her friend had only just thought of it for her benefit, she couldn't accept. 'Honestly, Molly, you don't need to take Tim. He's no trouble,' she said.

But the boys had not been quite as absorbed in their game as their mother thought. 'A trip to the swimming baths. Great!' David exclaimed. 'Let Tim come with us, please, Mrs Delaney.'

Both Molly and Tim added their pleas to David's and Helen laughed, throwing up her hands in mock despair. 'Okay, okay.' She turned to her son. 'You can go providing you do exactly as Molly tells you.'

'He's a good lad,' Molly said with a smile. 'You don't need to worry, Helen.'

'I'll do as I'm told, honestly,' Tim promised.

'Here's the key then,' Helen said. 'Run along and fetch your trunks and a towel and change those dirty jeans and that T-shirt whilst you're there.'

'Can I get a drink and a biscuit?' Tim shouted over his shoulder as he shot along the street.

Helen nodded her head. 'Yes, but hurry!' And then she turned to Molly. 'Thanks again, it's very kind of you.'

'Kind nothing,' Molly scoffed. 'David's much less trouble when he has Tim to play with him. It's pure selfishness on my part, so stop fretting, Helen. Just go home and put your feet up, forget your responsibilities. Read a book or watch television. Tim will be perfectly happy without you for a few hours.'

When Tim had gone Helen put the kettle on and then unpacked the picnic things, washing the cups and plastic plates and leaving the flask to soak in the sink. The kettle boiled just as she finished so she made a cup of tea and sat at the kitchen table to drink it, luxuriating in the peace and silence, enjoying the faintest of cool breezes wafting through the opened windows. The kitchen was a cheerful room, gleaming yellow tiles complementing the brown and white of the modern, streamlined units. The sun shone through the leaded glass windows in the mornings as they were eating their breakfast but just now it was cool and shadowed and Helen could feel the tensions of the day flowing out of her.

Molly was right, of course. She did need to relax. The doctor had told her, so had Philip. Unfortunately it was easier said than done. She couldn't escape from the past. Matt haunted her, day and night. She hadn't told anyone how she felt, not even Philip. Explanations were too painful at the moment. Perhaps they always would be. She drank the last of her tea and rinsed her cup under the tap, leaving it to drain. It was stupid to brood about Matt. It wouldn't change anything. It was too late. She had made her decision and now she had to live with it.

She picked up the paperback mystery she had borrowed from the library and headed for the stairs. She would do as Molly had suggested: take a long, cool bath and read a book. An unaccustomed luxury that in the past she would have unreservedly enjoyed. But today the ingenuity of Miss Marple failed to hold her interest and in the end she dropped the book on to the bathmat and simply lay back with her eyes closed, her brain as empty of thought as a zombie's.

She was still in the same torpid, mindless daze half an hour later when the door bell rang. At first she ignored the unwelcome interruption. If it was something important they would come again, she decided. But the ringing continued and she began to wonder whether it could be either Tim or Philip returning home unexpectedly early. Philip had gone to visit one of his old parishioners and it wouldn't be the first time he had forgotten to take his key. It was unlikely, she knew that, but once the idea had entered her head it became impossible to ignore. She clambered quickly out of the bath. She had already put out clean underwear and an old cotton sundress and she threw them on quickly now, not troubling to dry herself properly so that when she pattered down the stairs her bare feet left small, damp patches on the blue, flowered carpet.

The stairway led directly into the hall and she could see a man's dark shadow under the porch. An adult then—not Tim anyway, and too tall for Philip. She was already regretting her decision to answer the bell and she turned the key in the lock reluctantly. She ought to have peered out of the window to check the identity of the caller, she realised belatedly. She just didn't have the patience this evening to deal with one of the lame ducks that Philip collected so assiduously. His goodwill was boundless. It seemed to embrace everyone. He never refused to help, whatever the cost to his own peace of mind. But if this was another drunk come to cry on Philip's shoulder, Helen determined that she at least was going to slam the door immediately, whether Philip disapproved or not. She just couldn't cope, not today.

The man standing beside the pot of glowing geraniums had his back to Helen, his hands thrust carelessly in the pockets of cream, cotton slacks, watching a group of young children playing a noisy game of tug in the street. But as he turned very slowly to face her, Helen was assailed by a dreadful sense of *déjà vu*. This had all happened before at Fell Cottage. The shock of opening the door and finding Matt Seymour on the threshold. She clung desperately to the door handle, her legs trembling beneath her.

'Hello, Helen,' said Matt, very quietly, his eyes darkly intent. 'Aren't you going to ask me in?'

And she stepped backwards like someone in a dream, automatically widening the gap so that he could enter. 'The living room's through there. Please go in,' she stated in a cool, tight little voice so unlike her own. In fact she was totally stunned, left without even the presence of mind to close the door in Matt's handsome face. She followed him in and faced his tall figure across the comfortable, bronze dralon sofa. 'Why are you here?' she asked. Now that her numbed brain had started working again the pain of his presence in that small room was almost overwhelming.

'I could say that I was just passing, I suppose; saw the name of the street and dropped in on a purely friendly impulse.' He was staring at Helen as he spoke but his expression was far from friendly.

'Don't play games with me, Matt,' she replied, raising one shaking hand to cover her bare, white throat. 'I've had a long day. I'm tired. Say whatever you have to say and then just go and leave me alone.'

Matt's lips twisted slightly. 'What's the matter, Helen? Afraid your friend will come in unexpectedly and find us together?' he asked, his eyebrows winged in bitter mockery above dark-lashed eyes. 'Would he suspect the worst, I wonder?'

'Get out,' Helen whispered huskily, trying in vain to

stop her voice from trembling. 'I don't have to stand and listen to this. We're not at Ellermere now, Matt. This is Philip's house and you're not welcome here.'

'Knock you about a bit, would he, if he knew I'd been?' Matt replied, still watching her face intently.

'Just go! Don't say any more! I shan't listen to you if you do,' Helen exclaimed, gripping the back of the sofa for support. Her legs were trembling so much she was afraid that if he didn't leave soon she would collapse in an ignominious heap at his feet. And now more than ever she was determined he wouldn't guess just how much he could disturb her. Clearly she had been mistaken in her reading of his character. He was far from being the kind, considerate individual she had always imagined him. He was a cruel, heartless beast. He had done nothing but mock her since he walked through the door.

'I've no intention of leaving until I have said what I came to say,' he told her now abruptly.

She shook her head helpless, in the face of his determination. 'Say it quickly then, whatever it is!'

'Does he beat you, Helen?' he asked again in a hard, grim voice, the mockery entirely missing from his face.

'No! No, of course not,' Helen cried. 'Oh, just go, Matt! It's obvious you haven't anything of importance to say to me. I don't know why you've come.'

'This is why, Helen.' Matt took a step forward and she retreated instinctively, her back against the door. Matt stopped abruptly, looking grimmer than ever. 'Don't worry, I'm not going to touch you,' he said. 'But I received a letter yesterday and I think you ought to read it.'

Helen's hand shook as she took the envelope from Matt's fingers. 'It's Tim's writing.' She raised her eyes, a nasty, sick feeling invading the pit of her stomach. 'I knew nothing about this. Why has Tim written to you?'

'Open the envelope and read what he has to say,' he instructed harshly. 'It isn't very long but I think you will be interested.'

She bent her head, stray curls falling over her forehead, her fingers shaking as she took the paper out of the envelope. She was almost afraid to look. Whatever Tim had said it had brought Matt running. It had to be something startling. Her eyes flickered over Tim's large, neatly formed writing. She turned the page, feeling the colour draining out of her cheeks.

'How could he? Oh, how could he?' she breathed at last, more to herself than to Matt. She had been afraid that Tim had written asking Matt to fetch him back to Ellermere. But this was worse, far worse.

'Is it true, Helen? Does Ackroyd beat you both?'

'No, no, of course he doesn't. Philip has never hit me in his life—or Tim.' She put a hand to her forehead, distractedly trying to think. What could have possessed Tim to write a letter like this? Telling such unforgivable lies.

'You're still here, so I assume that whatever he has done you still love him and you are willing to forgive him. That's your business, of course,' he told her harshly. 'But if you think I'm going to allow him to hit my son again, you are very much mistaken.'

At first Matt's words didn't register. Helen was still gazing down at Tim's letter in a shocked daze, but very slowly she lifted her head. 'What did you say?' she whispered.

'You know perfectly well what I said, Helen,' he answered, his voice rasping angrily. He had moved nearer and he seemed to loom over her, his eyes blazing down into hers with almost physical force.

If Helen had been pale before she was like a ghost now. She moved her head distractedly, a trembling hand pressed to her eyes. 'I—I'm sorry. I shall have to sit down. I think I'm going to faint,' she said.

But he ignored her tremulous words, reaching out with cruel fingers to grip her shoulders. 'Tim is my son, isn't he, Helen?' he demanded fiercely. 'Answer me, damn you! Answer me!'

She tried to speak, she felt her lips move but her throat was constricted with shock and panic and no words came out.

He shook her fiercely, her body as helpless as a rag doll in his grasp. 'Tell the truth for once, you deceitful little bitch! It is the truth, isn't it?' he said through his teeth, shaking her again. 'I went to the States and saw Steven soon after you left Ellermere. He told me you had never been lovers. I believed him, Helen!'

She swayed in his cruel gasp, lowering her pale lids so that she didn't need to see the rage, the bitterness, the fierce contempt in his eyes. 'I told you the same thing but you didn't believe me,' she managed to whisper.

'If you had told me the truth. If you had reminded me of the night Dave Thornton tampered with my drinks and I drove you home, then I would have believed you,' he said.

And she trembled in his arms, her lashes flickering upwards as she gazed at him in shock. He was no longer guessing at the truth. He had remembered. It was useless trying to deny it any longer.

Matt was watching her intently, his lips twisted into a small, bitter smile. 'When I came here today, I wasn't completely sure, I still had a few faint doubts, but believe me, Helen, one look at your face and they have completely vanished.'

'You're wrong,' Helen whispered shakily, but clearly he didn't believe her.

'Damn you! Don't try to evade the truth any longer.

Haven't you done enough damage? Haven't you caused enough pain? Perhaps I can't remember everything but I remember enough, believe me! I remember the feel of you in my arms. I remember kissing you,' he told her, his voice deepening, the anger and contempt fading from his eyes as he added, 'I've dreamed about you for years, Helen. Since before you left Ellermere that first time. They were sensual, feverish dreams. I couldn't understand them. I told myself I was going crazy. I loved Natalie. I was going to marry her. You were just a child. Our relationship was that of brother and sister rather than lovers, but still I couldn't get you out of my head. You haunted my nights. It's only in the past few weeks that I've realised the truth. Realised that my dreams were in fact reality, my memories of that night, deeply buried. Tim is my son, isn't he, Helen?' And the hoarse intensity of his voice demanded an answer.

'Yes,' she whispered in anguish. 'Yes!'

'My God, how could you do it? How could you keep my son from me like this?' he cried. 'I would never have believed you could be so cruel. Hiding his birth was bad enough, but to let me get to know him, to love him, and then to take him away again. How could you, Helen?'

'I had no other choice,' Helen cried bitterly.

'You could have stayed at Ellermere! You could have married me!'

'Did you ask me, Matt? If you did, I'm afraid I never heard you,' she answered, tears springing to her eyes.

Matt was almost as pale as Helen, his fingers digging painfully into her shoulders again as he said hoarsely, 'Did I need to ask? A fool could have recognised how I felt about you. I loved you, Helen. You must have known that you only had to say the word and I would have married you.'

Helen's tremulous laugh was harsh with disbelief. She

had been right to keep Tim's birth secret from him. This was what she had feared all along. 'It's no use, Matt. I'm not a fool you see. I know you would never have mentioned marriage if it hadn't been for Tim. You had plenty of opportunity to ask me when we lived at Ellermere, but you never did!'

'God, Helen, I was afraid to ask! Surely you can see that.'

'Why should I believe you?' Helen scoffed.

'Because it's the truth, damn it! We were happy together. It wasn't enough for me, I'll admit that,' he said hoarsely. 'But it was better than nothing. I was afraid to upset the balance. I knew how you felt about Philip Ackroyd and I was afraid to put your feelings for me to the test.' He paused for a moment, shaking his head. 'I realised that Tim was my son weeks ago. If he was all I wanted why didn't I come to you then? Answer me that.'

There was a deep sincerity in Matt's voice that Helen found very difficult to ignore and yet she was afraid to trust such frail evidence. He wanted Tim, she knew that, but she couldn't believe that he loved her as well. 'I don't believe you. I can't believe you,' she faltered.

'You don't want to believe me,' said Matt angrily. 'You want an excuse to stay here with Philip Ackroyd. Well, damn it, Helen, I'm not going to allow you to do so. If necessary I shall call the police, insist that a doctor examines both you and my son. I've let you go too easily before, thinking you would only despise me if I begged you to stay. But I ought never to have allowed you to leave Ellermere. I see that now. I ought to have held you there by force if necessary.'

And before Helen could react he had taken her in his arms, looking down into her pale, shocked face with glittering eyes. 'You won't escape from me so easily again,' he muttered and then he was kissing her fiercely, hungrily, the kiss deepening, bruising her lips as though the feel of her body in his arms, her mouth under his own, had banished the last of his self-control. When he raised his head at last Helen leaned against him weakly, in shocked reaction, the blood turning to fire in her veins, her whole body trembling.

'I love you! I love you!' he groaned, his mouth against her forehead. 'Take pity on me, Helen. I know you don't feel the same but I'm not a fool, I know that physically at least I can make you respond to me. The rest will come. I swear I'll make you happy.' But then his voice broke on a small, self-derisive laugh. He lifted his head, his face pale. 'God, what am I saying? One failed marriage behind me and I'm promising to make you happy. You must feel like laughing in my face.'

The bitterness in Matt's voice tore at Helen's heart. She was totally confused, still dazed from his fierce kisses. In the past weeks she had ceased to hope. She had buried the emotion deep in her breast, and now it was a shock to feel the frail, tentative shoots growing again inside her.

'You loved Natalie, I know that,' she whispered.

His arms tightened around her and he looked deep into her eyes. 'No, I never loved her, Helen. I swear I never felt like this about her. Not for a moment. She was beautiful and I desired her,' he admitted quietly. 'And I simply wasn't mature enough to recognise the absence of love. Within weeks of the marriage I knew I had made a mistake. I don't even know whether Natalie ever loved me but I do know that after Katy was born and she found someone else, I didn't even care any longer.'

Helen closed her eyes tightly. 'That's why you never talked about her. Oh Matt, I've been such a fool.' There were tears trembling on the ends of her lashes but maybe her tremulous, parted lips told their own story because Matt cupped her chin with one possessive hand.

'Oh God, Helen, I adore you,' he muttered unsteadily and then he was kissing her again, a deep, hungry kiss which made her head spin, her arms sliding around his shoulders, stroking his neck with restless, searching fingers. Salt tears were trickling slowly down her cheeks and he kissed them away, covering her eyes, her mouth, the smooth sweep of cheek and jawline with his eager lips. Helen clung to him helplessly, still not quite sure whether she was dreaming. He hadn't loved Natalie after all. She could hardly believe it was true, but his kisses were real enough and the unsteady thud of his heart against her breast.

At last he raised his head and the expression in his eyes made her heart turn over. 'Put me out of my misery, Helen,' he whispered hoarsely, stroking her cheek with one shaking hand. 'Say you'll come home with me. We can't manage without you, none of us. Katy—my mother—we all want you back.'

The time for doubts, the time for lies had passed, Helen realised. For once in her life she had to take a chance. She had to trust. She had to tell the absolute truth. 'I love you,' she whispered. 'I've always loved you.' She saw his face and added, 'I thought you were still in love with Natalie. I thought that was why no one ever mentioned her name.'

'You idiot. You crazy, little idiot,' Matt whispered on a deep, husky note. 'Why did you leave Ellermere? Why did you leave me if that was how you felt?'

'Like you, I was afraid,' Helen confessed. 'I didn't want you to pity me. Because I was sure you still loved Natalie, I didn't want to be second best.'

'Never, Helen,' he told her hoarsely. 'You never have been second best. You never could be. I've loved you for months. You're all I've thought about, all I've dreamed of. These last weeks have been hell, imagining you in Philip Ackroyd's bed, thinking that you still loved him. You will never know how pleased I was to receive Tim's letter. At last I had an excuse to come and see you, to try and persuade you to come home with me. I'll make you forget him, Helen,' he promised. 'I swear I will.' And Helen stood on tiptoe, smiling gently as she kissed him very swiftly on the mouth. But when he tried to return her embrace, she pulled out of his arms.

'Not yet,' she said, still smiling. 'I want to show you something.' And she took his hand, pulling him across the room towards the old-fashioned sideboard. Matt was looking not only puzzled but faintly worried as well and she picked up a silver framed photograph and handed it to him quickly. 'Do you recognise anyone, Matt?' she asked.

He was still frowning as he bent his head. He shot her a sideways glance. 'Your Aunt Lily,' he said. 'But I don't recognise the elderly, clerical gentleman by her side.'

'It's her wedding photograph,' Helen said simply. 'She married Philip Ackroyd three years before her death and she was his housekeeper before that. Now do you understand?'

He was still clutching the photograph in one hand, staring down at it like a man in an advanced state of shock. 'This man is Philip Ackroyd?' he asked and she nodded.

'There was never anyone but you, Matt, I promise. I lied to you in the past but I'm telling the truth now. You must believe me.'

'I ought to shake the life out of you,' he exclaimed, but there was no anger in his voice and his eyes were smiling warmly into hers. He put the photograph down on the sideboard and held out his arms. 'Come here Helen Delaney and let me punish you as you deserve,' he said.

She shook her head. 'Helen Morley, I was never married. That was another lie,' she confessed, hanging back.

'Never mind the irrelevancies,' Matt said, reaching out and grabbing her shoulders. 'You're the future Mrs Seymour now, and as far as I'm concerned that's all that counts.'

'Are you sure, Matt?' Helen asked, her expression still faintly anxious. 'There's bound to be gossip, unpleasantness. People will remember that Aunt Lily was once a servant at Ellermere. There's no point in pretending that they won't.'

'To hell with that,' Matt said roughly, pulling her closer. 'If there are individuals with such tiny minds, I can only feel sorry for them. I love you. My family love you. As far as I am concerned no one else matters,' he said with unconscious arrogance.

'But what about Tim?' Helen murmured anxiously, her hands still pressed against his chest, holding him away. 'How do we explain his likeness to you?'

Matt gave a small laugh. 'I think the time has come to tell Tim the truth, my darling. My mother and Katy too, or at least as much of the truth as they can understand. As for the rest of the world,' he shrugged faintly, 'I imagine they will put two and two together fairly quickly and come to something approaching the truth. But it will be a nine days wonder, Helen. You'll see. I shall adopt Tim so that he is legally my son and eventually people will forget.'

'Oh, Matt,' Helen whispered. 'You make it sound so very simple.'

He laughed again, taking advantage of her momentary lack of concentration to pull her closer, bending his head to bury his face in her curls. 'What could be more simple?' he murmured. 'Say that you'll marry me, Helen and then let me kiss you again.'

She smiled up at him mistily, no longer even pretending to resist. 'Yes, Matt, I'll marry you,' she said. He pulled her down on to the sofa and they were still sitting there and he was still kissing her when the front door opened and Tim rushed in.

'Uncle Matt! Uncle Matt!' he cried, throwing himself headlong into his father's arms, his face buried in Matt's neck. 'I knew you'd come. I knew you would,' he sobbed. If Helen had still been angry with him for writing the letter to Matt all desire to punish him would have fled as she watched him crying his heart out in Matt's arms.

'It's all right, son,' Matt was saying, his voice reassuringly gentle as Tim sobbed out incoherent apologies into his ear. 'I understand. I'm glad you wrote to me, don't worry.'

He looked across at Helen over Tim's head. 'We have something to tell you, your mother and I.'

Tim looked up, rubbing the back of one, slightly grubby hand across his wet eyes and Helen smiled at him, reaching out to touch his cheek, her head still in the warm, protective curve of Matt's shoulder. 'Tim darling,' she said and that was as far as she got before he interrupted her.

'You're getting married!' he cried. 'We thought you would, Katy and I. Oh Uncle Matt, I'm so happy!' And he threw his arms around his father's neck and burst into tears again, his head on Matt's shoulder.

Matt stroked his son's dark hair, his eyes fixed on Helen's face. 'I don't think we're going to have any problems with Tim, do you, my darling?'

She shook her head, smiling through her own tears. 'He loves you, Matt. We both do. You won't have any problems with either of us, I promise you.'

The silver birch trees in the churchyard had turned to swaying gold the day Helen became Mrs Seymour. All the trees were bearing their autumn colour. The leaves had only just started to drop, looking like small piles of brown, red and orange paper, blown by the wind to lie against the ivy-covered walls. It had been raining during the night but in the middle of the morning the clouds had miraculously parted to reveal a sky of the palest egg-shell blue.

Helen was wearing a suit of ivory satin, slim-fitting with an elegant mandarin collar, the skirt flaring as it reached her knees. Katy, her only bridesmaid, was in pink, with a delicate wreath of rosebuds peeping through her dark curls. Helen could see her now, jumping up and down excitedly as she waited with Madeline Seymour in the church porch. Philip was waiting, too, his white hair shining silver in the autumn sunshine, his hand steadying her arm as she stepped carefully out of the Rolls on to the mossy pathway. She smiled up at him, sliding her arm through his.

'You look beautiful, my dear,' he murmured. 'I don't believe I have ever seen a lovelier bride.' And his eyes behind the thick spectacles were glowing with pride. Helen squeezed his arm tightly but she was too choked with emotion to answer him. The bells in the church tower had started to peal the moment she stepped out of the car and she could hear the organist beginning the triumphant notes of the wedding march.

Slowly they began to walk up the path towards the church and Helen lifted her head, smiling at the people from the village who had come to see the bride. Any doubts she had had in the past were banished. Matt loved her, and she him. To Helen this moment was the culmination of ten long years of waiting. Perhaps she had made a mistake hiding the truth from Matt all those years ago, but it was impossible to tell. They had both changed out of all recognition in the last ten years. Both had lived through a long spell of unhappiness and undoubtedly it had matured them. If they had married before Tim was born maybe she would have made him even more unhappy than Natalie had done. And certainly Katy would never have been born, and that would have been a pity, Helen thought, smiling now as Matt's daughter rushed headlong out of the porch towards her, dark curls and pink ribbons flying as she clutched at Helen's hand.

'You look beautiful, Aunty Helen,' she cried. 'Just like a fairy princess.'

'My dear.' Mrs Seymour had followed Katy and both her hands were held out in welcome. She squeezed Helen's fingers, her eyes unashamedly filled with tears. 'You look so happy.' She turned her head, smiling. 'Doesn't she, Philip?'

'Radiant,' Philip agreed, his own voice husky with emotion.

'Can we go in now? Daddy's waiting,' Katy cried.

Mrs Seymour gathered herself together with an obvious effort. 'Walk slowly along behind Helen, darling,' she said to Katy. 'And carry her bouquet when she hands it to you.' She kissed Helen's cheeks gently. 'Be happy, my dear,' she whispered. And then she turned and hurried down the aisle towards her seat at the front of the church.

The organ music swelled into a triumphant crescendo. Helen's heart was beating so quickly that she was afraid it would burst.

'Shall we go,' Philip said, smiling, his eyes warmly reassuring as they rested on her pale features. His smile deepened as he added, 'Ten years is long enough to keep any man waiting, don't you think?'

Helen laughed shakily. 'Oh Philip, I do love you,' she whispered.

He patted her fingers where they lay on his arm. 'That's good, because I love you too,' he said, and then they began to walk slowly up the aisle. The small church was crowded. Dimly Helen saw familiar faces turning to smile at her. Mr and Mrs Williams, Molly, with David grinning beside her. Tim was there of course, sitting beside Mrs Seymour and Steven's American wife. She was almost afraid to raise her head and look at the tall man standing in front of the altar. But Matt had no such inhibitions. He had turned the moment she entered the church and now he was striding towards her, Philip relinquishing her arm into his hand without a murmur. Matt raised her fingers to his lips and kissed them, his dark eyes never leaving her own.

'Helen, darling, you look beautiful. I love you,' he said deeply and in front of a very appreciative audience. Helen reached up, one hand on his shoulder and kissed him warmly on the mouth.

'Let's go and get married, Mr Seymour,' she whispered.

And they did.

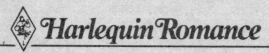

Harlequin Romance

Coming Next Month

2773 SHADOWS OF EDEN Rosemary Badger
Meeting a handsome wealthy author is just what the
survivor of an accident that claimed her family needed—
until her feelings turn to love and he starts to pull away.

2774 SAND CASTLES Meg Dominique
The manager of Florida's Hotel Fandango is ready to settle
down, while his ladylove doesn't dare stay in one place
long enough to get involved. Yet when he holds her in his
arms anything seems possible.

2775 AGE OF CONSENT Victoria Gordon
Despite the crush she once had on him, an out-of-work
journalist turns to a writer in Tasmania for help—only to
find that he and his beautiful girlfriend add to her worries.

2776 POWER POINT Rowan Kirby
A child psychologist puts her heart at risk when she breaks
all her rules of professional detachment in order to help a
dynamic documentary producer reach his young brother.

2777 BLUEBELLS ON THE HILL Barbara McMahon
In the peaceful Sierra Nevada, a rancher, still bitter over the
desertion of his wife, opens up to a woman who can't tell
him she isn't exactly what she seems.

2778 RETURN TO FARAWAY Valerie Parv
A film producer returns to the Australian Outback at her
estranged husband's invitation. Or so she thinks. But his
resentful teenage daughter from a previous marriage is up
to her old tricks!

Available in July wherever paperback books are sold, or
through Harlequin Reader Service.

In the U.S.
901 Fuhrmann Blvd.
P.O. Box 1397
Buffalo, N.Y. 14240-1397

In Canada
P.O. Box 2800, Postal Station A
5170 Yonge Street
Willowdale, Ontario M2N 6J3

Can you keep a secret?

You can keep this one plus 4 free novels

One of America's best-selling romance authors writes
her most thrilling novel!

TWIST OF FATE

JAYNE ANN KRENTZ

Hannah inherited the anthropological papers that could
bring her instant fame. But will she risk her life and give
up the man she loves to follow the family tradition?

Available in June at your favorite retail outlet, or reserve your copy for
May shipping by sending your name, address, and zip or postal code
along with a check or money order for $4.70 (includes 75¢ for postage
and handling) payable to Worldwide Library Reader Service to:

In the U.S.
Worldwide Library
901 Fuhrmann Blvd.
Buffalo, NY
14269

In Canada
Worldwide Library
P.O. Box 2800, 5170 Yonge St.
Postal Station A, Willowdale, Ont.
M2N 6J3

BPA—TOF-H-1

 WORLDWIDE LIBRARY®